The Cowboy's Secret Bride

By Cora Seton

Author's Note

The Cowboy's Secret Bride is the first volume in the Turners v. Coopers series. To find out more, look for the rest of the books in the series, including:

The Cowboy's Outlaw Bride (Volume 2)
The Cowboy's Hidden Bride (Volume 3)
The Cowboy's Stolen Bride (Volume 4)
The Cowboy's Forbidden Bride (Volume 5)

Also, don't miss Cora Seton's Chance Creek series, the Cowboys of Chance Creek, the Heroes of Chance Creek, the Brides of Chance Creek, and the SEALs of Chance Creek:

The Cowboys of Chance Creek Series:

The Cowboy Inherits a Bride (Volume 0)
The Cowboy's E-Mail Order Bride (Volume 1)
The Cowboy Wins a Bride (Volume 2)
The Cowboy Imports a Bride (Volume 3)
The Cowgirl Ropes a Billionaire (Volume 4)
The Sheriff Catches a Bride (Volume 5)
The Cowboy Lassos a Bride (Volume 6)
The Cowboy Rescues a Bride (Volume 7)
The Cowboy Earns a Bride (Volume 8)
The Cowboy's Christmas Bride (Volume 9)

The Heroes of Chance Creek Series:

The Navy SEAL's E-Mail Order Bride (Volume 1)
The Soldier's E-Mail Order Bride (Volume 2)
The Marine's E-Mail Order Bride (Volume 3)
The Navy SEAL's Christmas Bride (Volume 4)
The Airman's E-Mail Order Bride (Volume 5)

The Brides of Chance Creek Series:

Issued to the Bride One Navy SEAL
Issued to the Bride One Airman
Issued to the Bride One Sniper
Issued to the Bride One Marine
Issued to the Bride One Soldier

The SEALs of Chance Creek Series:

A SEAL's Oath
A SEAL's Vow
A SEAL's Pledge
A SEAL's Consent
A SEAL's Purpose
A SEAL's Resolve
A SEAL's Devotion
A SEAL's Desire
A SEAL's Struggle
A SEAL's Triumph

Visit Cora's website at www.coraseton.com
Find Cora on Facebook at facebook.com/CoraSeton
Sign up for my newsletter HERE.
www.coraseton.com/sign-up-for-my-newsletter

Chapter One

THIS WASN'T THE place.

Carl Whitfield swept his gaze across the pastures before him, took in the squat, ugly house perched close by, and shook his head over the dilapidated barns and outbuildings some distance away.

"Hilltop Acres is a bargain," Megan Lawrence, his realtor, said. An earnest young woman, she'd inherited him as a client when his former realtor, the senior partner at the firm, had given up on ever finding him a suitable property.

"It's small," he countered.

"It's a ranch. Not many of them for sale around here."

"You're telling me." He'd been searching for years. Three years, to be exact. He could picture what the right place would look like. A big house perched on a rise of ground, the land sloping away to a tremendous view. Plenty of acreage for a large cattle operation.

Not a stunted little spread like this one.

A prosperous ranch like the ones featured in the movies he used to watch with his father when he was young. His dad had spent summers in Montana when he was a kid. Loved to watch westerns and chew over old times.

"If you're not interested, we'd better leave. I've got another appointment." Megan pulled out her cell phone, frowned at something on the screen and tucked it away again.

Carl adjusted his hat. Back when his father was alive, he'd never dreamed he'd amass the means to buy a ranch. Now he wished his dad was here to help him pick one out. "Someone else is looking at this property?"

"No—it's Camila Torres. She just wants a little place in town."

"Camila—?" Carl cut off, his chest tightening. "Camila's looking for a house?"

"That's right. Two bedrooms, one bath. Close to her restaurant."

He bit back a curse. He'd blown his chance with Camila a long time ago, but he'd hoped—

Hell, he'd hoped she'd give him a little while longer to fulfill the terms of her ultimatum. He'd known since the moment he'd met her she was the one for him, and at one time he'd been sure she felt the same way, but he'd blown it on their first real date. He'd gone too far, too fast. Instead of keeping to light topics and getting-to-know-you conversation, he'd found himself talking about marriage, family, and his plans for the future.

Camila had listened gravely, and told him she had one requirement for the man she married.

He had to commit to staying in Chance Creek.

It was a simple thing. Yet he'd hesitated to say he would—for a number of reasons. He hadn't found a spread yet, he'd still had business in California that kept him flying back there frequently—and he'd still been too new to the community to feel secure in his place here. After all, his first attempt to settle in Chance Creek hadn't gone so well.

He'd regretted that hesitation ever since.

"Carl, I like you—a lot," Camila had said. "But I'm serious about this."

"I'm looking for a ranch," he'd told her.

"Ask me out again when you've bought one. Then I'll know you mean to stay."

"I hear some women like to pick out their home," he'd teased her.

"Feel free to ask my opinion, but I'm not taking this any farther until you've settled here."

"It's only a matter of time, I promise." Off-balance from the turn the conversation had taken, Carl hoped they could move on and enjoy the evening, but Camila had kept a polite distance for the remainder of the date. Carl, accepting the challenge she'd laid out for him, had redoubled his efforts to find a place. God knew he wanted to live here. Had wanted it for decades, ever since his father had first described the community. His dad hadn't summered here—he'd stayed with his great-uncle who'd had a small spread much nearer to Bozeman—but family friends had owned a much larger ranch in Chance Creek at the time. Carl's dad had considered it paradise. When Carl came to check out the town, he did too.

Unfortunately, finding a ranch here had proved impossible. He and Camila had drifted apart, until one day he realized he was avoiding her—and she was avoiding him. Things between them had gotten uncomfortable. His lack of progress made it look like he wasn't interested in her. That wasn't the case, and Carl didn't know how it had come to this.

"Is Camila dating anyone?" he asked Megan, focusing on the present.

Megan shot him a curious look. "Not that I know of. She works too much to date."

Carl nodded. That was Camila. She'd told him she'd spent every dime opening her restaurant with her partner, Fila Matheson. She wanted to build up her savings again. She'd set down roots—and she didn't want anything to be able to dislodge her again.

He wanted that too. Always had.

But he'd begun to feel that his hesitation three years ago had cursed him. He hadn't confirmed his desire to stay quickly enough, and ever since, Chance Creek kept rejecting him. Every time a suitable property came up for sale, someone bought it right out from under his nose.

If Camila purchased a home, it would sink the final nail in his coffin. He'd have to admit he'd blown it. She'd have made her own home in Chance Creek.

Without him.

He scanned the property again. It was small, but it was a working ranch. The house was a hovel—but he could rebuild.

"Carl? You coming?" Megan asked, already walking away.

"Yeah. Listen, I want to make an offer. First thing tomorrow," he added when the realtor turned in surprise. He needed to talk to Camila first.

"Really?" Megan asked.

"Really." He was done screwing around. Done waiting to start his life as a rancher.

Done standing by while Camila moved on without him.

He'd hesitated once—and lost his chance to be with her.

He sure as hell wasn't going to let that happen again.

THIS WASN'T THE place.

Camila tried to hide her disappointment as Megan extolled the virtues of a kitchen so small its oven and fridge were three-quarter size. The house's two bedrooms had been hardly big enough to hold beds. It lacked hookups for a washer and dryer. The living room faced north, gloomy as a crypt on this beautiful spring morning.

It wasn't going to work.

"It's in your budget," Megan reminded her when she was done praising the scant two feet of chipped counter-top.

"I guess I was hoping for something... more."

She was hoping for something that felt like home, but all this place did was remind her that since leaving

Houston she might have started a business and made some great friends, but her situation was still temporary. Someday one of the Turners would want the cabin she rented from them. Then what would she do? She'd scraped together a down payment that would barely get her into a house like this, but the truth was, she'd pictured something altogether different when she'd thought of buying a home.

Something bigger.

Prettier.

Something she wouldn't move into alone.

She'd never thought she'd still be single when she went house-hunting. Once she'd even thought she'd found the man she wanted to be with—

But Carl hadn't been ready to settle down. He hadn't even been able to say if he planned to stay in Chance Creek. For all his promises that he'd buy a ranch soon, he never had.

He had stayed, though. Camila saw him all the time, and it was like torture having him so close—and knowing he wasn't the one for her. She knew she'd done the right thing, though, cutting off contact with him.

Leaving Houston had nearly killed her. Striking out on her own after a lifetime at the heart of her big, boisterous family had been like stepping into an abyss— not knowing where she'd land, or if she'd survive.

She'd done well for herself since. Started her own business. Found wonderful friends. She was staying right here, for good. She needed a man as committed to

Chance Creek as she was.

Or maybe she needed to be alone. Camila was beginning to think that staying in Chance Creek and having a partner in life were mutually exclusive.

"Are you and Carl an item?" Megan asked.

Camila swung around to stare at her. "Me and Carl?" Had Megan read her mind?

"He asked about you this morning. I didn't know you two were friends."

He'd asked about her?

Camila couldn't say why the thought left her breathless. It wasn't like she still carried a torch for him after all this time. He obviously didn't carry one for her. He was polite when they met. He was still living in a cabin on the Cooper spread. No closer than he'd been three years ago to buying a place of his own.

She pictured the handsome cowboy in this kitchen, bumping against the counter in the too-small space, trying to maneuver around the table she'd have to add. He wouldn't fit.

Which didn't matter. Carl would never be in this house.

Camila gave herself a mental shake. She had to make decisions based on reality, not fantasy, but she heard herself say, "I—uh—I don't think this house is for me."

Megan sighed. "Let's see what else we can find."

CARL'S FOOT TAPPED as he waited in line at the Chance Creek Spring Fling fair later that afternoon for a chance to talk to Camila, who was turning skewers of chicken on the grill in the food tent in front of him. Pent up energy made him restless. It was riling him up to wait rather than just put in that offer on Hilltop Acres. He'd gotten skunked not once, but several times before when he hadn't moved fast enough to purchase a place. He wasn't the only one desperate for a ranch around here.

He had to win out this time, but he had to talk to Camila first. While he did, he'd grab some of her delicious butter chicken nachos, which he'd been craving.

He ached to steal a kiss, too. As soon as he'd given himself leave to think about pursuing Camila again, all his desire for her had flooded back. He'd been keeping it at bay through sheer doggedness. That wasn't working anymore.

Unfortunately, Maya Turner was also manning the booth. She'd taken to helping Camila and Fila on festival days. With the Turner/Cooper feud as hot as the eighty-five-degree temperatures that had nudged Chance Creek into an early summer, everyone knew it would only take one spark to really set off a blaze between the families. Last week there'd been a minor altercation at the Dancing Boot between Liam Turner and Lance Cooper.

He'd have to watch what he said in front of Maya. No one needed another fight on a day like this.

By the time he made it to the counter of the concession stand, where Maya manned the till under a large white canopy, Carl was starving. And hot. A trickle of sweat made its way between his shoulder blades under his black cotton T-shirt.

"I'll have a plate of those butter chicken nachos," he told Maya when it was his turn to order.

Fila came to deliver a plate of food to another customer, flipped her long black braid over her shoulder and said, "Hey, Carl. How are you doing?" She was sensibly dressed in a light cotton sundress.

"Pretty terrific."

Fila raised her eyebrows at his enthusiasm. "Finally found a ranch?" she quipped.

Hell. It was no secret he'd been looking for a long time, but he glanced at Maya, hoping she didn't know why he needed one so badly. "Actually, yeah, I did."

Fila blinked in surprise, leaned closer and asked, "Does that mean you'll finally ask her out?" She lowered her voice nearly to a whisper. "Camila's wasting her life waiting for you."

Carl winced. He wasn't trying to waste Camila's life. Still, if Fila thought she was still waiting for him, that was good news. Maybe all his worries were for nothing.

"Ask who out?" Maya chirped, leaning closer, too. "Who does Carl want to date?"

Camila looked up from the grill, caught Carl's gaze, blushed and swiftly looked away.

Carl's body reacted immediately to that blush, and he wanted to vault the table and go straight to her. Instead he cleared his throat and sent Fila a pointed look. "No one."

Fila had the grace to look chagrined. It wouldn't do for Maya to learn about his history with Camila—or the attraction that simmered between them still.

At least on his side.

Carl dipped his head and glanced Camila's way under the brim of his hat. She was doing a good job pretending not to notice the conversation, but he knew she was listening. She was still flushed, her mouth pinched in a thin line. He wished like hell Maya wasn't here—it was impossible to tell if Camila's reaction was due to the presence of the Turner or because she'd decided she would rather Carl never found a ranch at all. After all, according to Megan, she was looking for a house of her own.

"I've been doing what needed to be done," he told Fila, loudly enough for Camila to hear. "A promise is a promise." He hoped they both understood what he meant.

Camila glanced up again. Caught his eye. Looked away with a shake of her head.

Carl's gut tightened. What did that mean?

"A promise is stupid if you ask me," Fila said just as loudly. "You're lucky no one else came along to steal her heart."

"Who's heart?" Maya asked. "And why are you all yelling?"

Carl gripped the edge of the counter. No one had better be chasing after Camila. He was still trying to process that head shake. Was she telling him to stop talking about it in front of Maya? Or was she telling him she wasn't interested anymore?

"It could happen, you know," Fila asserted.

He did know. Camila was something special. He was amazed she'd waited this long for him to get it together, and sometimes he worried another man would snatch her up before he could find what he was looking for.

"Who. Are. You. Talking. About?" Maya demanded.

Carl paid for his order and stepped aside to wait for his food without answering her, and Maya let out a little huff. "Coopers," she said derisively.

"Carl's not a Cooper," Fila told her.

"He might as well be. He worships them. And he acts like them, too. Stubborn as a mule."

Carl kept his cool. He'd never understood the feud between the two families, or how someone as level-headed as Maya could fall under its sway.

But all the Turners were like that. Dead set against the Coopers. And vice versa. Had been for years.

While Carl waited, he kept his eye on Camila, but she never once looked up to meet his gaze. He knew she got a great deal on rent from the Turners and wouldn't want to put that in jeopardy just to chat with him—not until he'd bought his ranch and made it clear he meant to stay.

When Fila delivered his meal, Maya turned to speak with another customer, and suddenly Camila straightened. She caught his eye. "Ten minutes," she mouthed and pointed in the direction of the portable toilets set a discreet distance away from the rest of the festivities, then turned back to her grill so fast Carl thought he might have hallucinated the whole thing.

But he hadn't. His pulse kicked up as he walked

away from the booth. Camila wanted to meet with him. Talk to him.

The portable toilets might not be his first choice as a rendezvous spot, but who cared?

This was his chance to move things forward with Camila—and he meant to make the most of it.

He'd only made it about twenty paces away from the food tent, however, when something sharp prodded him in the side.

"Carl!"

"Hell!" Carl nearly dropped his nachos as a gimlet-eyed, gray-haired woman poked the tip of her umbrella into his rib cage again. He sidestepped her third attempt to spear him. "Virginia—you nearly made me lose my food!"

Carl's anger didn't faze her. Nothing fazed Virginia Cooper, matriarch of the Cooper clan, and his landlord at Thorn Hill. Since he'd moved onto the spread, he'd come to enjoy the younger generation of Coopers, despite their ready tempers, but Virginia was another matter. Virginia would try the patience of a saint. It wasn't her age—her 84 years hadn't slowed down her keen acumen, her fast stride, or her sharp tongue.

She was simply mean.

Carl had learned to stay out of her way.

"I've got a proposition for you!" she announced, ignoring his protest. "Did you hear about the prize?" In her three-quarter length gray skirt and flower-patterned blouse, Virginia was neat as a pin. Her gray hair was pulled back, braided and coiled into a bun. Her fingers gleamed with several large rings, but none of them circled her ring finger. Virginia had never married.

"What prize?" Carl looked back to catch a glimpse of Camila but too many people blocked his view.

"What prize? Weren't you paying attention to the announcements? It's only the biggest piece of news to hit Chance Creek in over a hundred years!"

Now she had his attention. "What's going on?"

"The city's giving up Settler's Ridge. Giving it away to the winner—which will be us!" Virginia's eyes shone with determination.

Carl was lost. "Where's Settler's Ridge? And how would we win it?"

She poked him again with her umbrella. "Settler's Ridge is a ranch that straddles Pittance Creek to the north of Thorn Hill and the Flying W. It was given to the city by the Ridleys in 1962, and kept in trust since then. Those fools thought the town center would spread to encompass it. Must have figured Chance Creek was the next Chicago." She shook her head to show what she thought of that. "It's been sitting there unused ever since."

Carl was beginning to understand the significance of the announcement. If the Coopers won it, they could double the size of their ranch.

"Think of it." Virginia jabbed with the umbrella, but Carl dodged it. "Twice the land—and control over Pittance Creek," she said triumphantly.

Clarity crashed over him. There was the rub. The land was one thing, but the water could be even more important. The Turners' ranch—the Flying W—depended on Pittance Creek, too. Both ranches had wells, of course, but the creek was valuable, nonetheless.

"Virginia, you're incorrigible. You wouldn't deprive the Turners of their water, would you?"

"Maybe. Maybe not. Depends."

Hell, he wanted no part of this. "Well, good luck. Hope you win."

"That's all you've got to say?" Virginia lifted her chin. "Fat lot of help you are, after everything we've done for you."

Carl sighed. "What do you have to do to win it?" he asked, going along with the conversation, but promising himself his involvement would end with it. He needed to focus on Camila—and buying Hilltop Acres.

"Provide the biggest boost to civic life during the next six months. Whatever that means."

Carl could have laughed. It meant the Coopers would have to do something good for the town at large—maybe for the first time in their lives. The family wasn't known for its civic-mindedness. "Like I said, good luck." This time Carl really meant it. If vying to win Settler's Ridge motivated them to become model citizens, he was all for it. He liked the Coopers, but they were a wild bunch.

"That's where you come in."

"What do you mean?" Carl nearly groaned. He should have known she'd try to rope him into something. His eyes wandered to watch Camila working again. He couldn't help it.

He yelped at a sharp pain in his ribs. "Hey!" He eyed Virginia and her pointy-tipped umbrella.

"Pay attention. This is important. Like I said, I've got a proposition for you."

"Spit it out!"

"You help me win this contest, and I'll help you get that ranch you want so badly. Must be getting old living in our little cabin. A millionaire like you," she added.

"You'll sell me Settler's Ridge?" That was interesting. He tried to picture the land to the north of Thorn Hill. All he'd seen from the road was a tangle of brush and scrub. Were there any buildings on it? He couldn't say. At least it was close to town.

Virginia bristled. "I'm not selling you Cooper land. I'm talking about another ranch. It's not for sale yet, but it will be soon. I can get you access to the seller before anyone else even knows about it. If—and only if—you help me win."

A ranch for sale no one knew about? That would be a miracle. Prosperous ranches in these parts stayed in family hands for generations. The ones that did come on the market were too dry, too rugged, too far from town, too one thing or another. Multiple buyers competed for them anyhow. Before today, he'd almost given up hope he'd ever find a decent place. Hilltop Acres barely qualified.

He didn't doubt Virginia's word, though. Despite being the nominal owner of Thorn Hill, she'd spent the last few years at the Prairie Garden assisted living facility in town, and that put her in close proximity with dozens of pensioners who might be ready to dispose of a property.

"If we get a jump on this civic stuff, no one will be able to catch us. Give my family a leg up, and I'll see you get your ranch," she said.

"You want me to donate money?" He supposed he could do that much. He could keep the ranch Virginia knew about in his hip pocket, in case something fell through with Hilltop Acres—or Camila vetoed it. He'd been meaning to contribute more here in Chance Creek. After all, this was his town, too.

At least, he meant it to be. He couldn't wait for the day he'd wrapped up all his business in California for good. Sven Andersson, an old friend and key employee, had asked Carl to invest in his startup when Carl sold off his own businesses. Carl had gladly said yes because Sven had come through for him a hundred times during his journey to becoming a millionaire, but investing rapidly turned into consulting, and that had turned into a nearly full-time gig. Despite what he'd promised to Camila about staying put, he'd ended up flying out to California an awful lot these past few years. He figured Sven had helped make him rich. The least he could do was return the favor. At least the company—Andersson Robotics—was doing quite well. Carl hoped the worst of it was in the past. He had to focus on Chance Creek now.

"Not just money," Virginia said. "The whole she-bang. We need to blow all the other contenders out of the water. Which means we need a killer idea. We'll take the town by storm and leave everyone else in the dirt."

Carl caught sight of Camila bending over the grill. She tucked a tendril of hair behind her ear…

Virginia kicked his shin.

"Hey!" Carl focused on the old woman again.

"Anyone can donate money to the town. We need to donate something big. Something everyone will remember forever."

"Like what?" His ten minutes were ticking away. He needed to shake Virginia.

"If I knew, I wouldn't be asking you for ideas." Virginia pursed her lips. "Something that goes back to our roots. We Coopers built Chance Creek's first elementary school in 1898, and every generation since has us to thank for their education. Maybe we'll build a new high school."

"The town already has a high school," Carl pointed out.

"And a sorrier piece of work I've never seen. The Turners were responsible for that travesty. Now the roof leaks in a dozen places, the auditorium is much too small and it's ugly."

Carl frowned. If Virginia tried to tear down a Turner building and replace it with a Cooper one, the two families would be fighting in the streets before construction even began. At the same time, he remembered a conversation he'd had with Sven recently about how the lack of technology in schools in poorer districts meant that kids were being left behind before they even graduated from high school. That gave him a better idea.

"Chance Creek doesn't need a new school. It needs a way to train its students for the future. You can fix up the current high school—and offer them a better education at the same time."

Virginia snorted. "You can gild a trash can, but it won't smell any better."

"Hear me out." Carl warmed to the idea. If he was going to give back to Chance Creek, this was a good way to start. "Schools these days are changing. They've got 3-D printers in the computer labs, tablets in classrooms, technology everywhere. The workplace is changing, too. Not all our students are going to be ranchers. The rest need to be ready to work in an automated world—and I doubt Chance Creek High is doing much in that regard. You could do something to fix that. Launch some kind of program that really sets our high school apart from the others."

"Like what?" Virginia sounded skeptical.

Carl thought about it. "You still need to repair the building. But once that's done, I'd look for an idea that makes people sit up and take notice." He thought of Sven again. "Like… robotics. That would get press like you wouldn't believe."

"Robotics, huh?" Virginia mused. "I like it. No one will see that coming." She nodded as if it had been settled. "I'll need the proposal next week."

"The proposal?"

"That's right."

"Next week?" Carl laughed but faltered when Virginia's chin lifted in anger. How had his role escalated from pitching possibilities to being in charge of the project? "Virginia, I'm just giving you ideas, remember?"

Virginia smacked her umbrella on the ground. "I thought you needed a ranch."

"I already found one. Going to put an offer in tomorrow." He'd like to help bring Chance Creek High into the twenty-first century, but he hadn't signed on to be Virginia's lackey.

Her eyes narrowed. "What ranch did you find?" she demanded.

"Hilltop Acres, over by—"

She snorted. "I guarantee you the ranch to which I'm referring is ten times what Hilltop Acres will ever be."

"Maybe so, but I can't wait around, because—" he remembered almost too late he couldn't tell Virginia about Camila "—I've already waited long enough," he finished lamely.

"But you haven't bought it yet?" Virginia watched him silently for a moment, and Carl couldn't begin to guess what she was thinking. "I have a feeling you'll come around," she said finally, then turned on her heel and walked away.

"I'M TAKING A short break," Camila told Fila and Maya when there was a lull in the traffic at the food tent. "Be back in a flash."

She quickly undid her apron and left it folded beside

the grill, then ducked out and made a beeline in the direction of the portable toilets on the far side of the fairgrounds. Not exactly her first choice of setting for a conversation with the man of her dreams, but definitely inconspicuous. She gave a tiny wave to Carl as she passed him. He was standing with his uneaten plate of nachos in his hand, watching Virginia Cooper stalk off toward the craft stalls. Camila kept walking, hoping Carl would follow.

She still couldn't believe he'd found a ranch. To be honest, she'd begun to think he'd stopped looking—that he'd long ago lost interest in her.

She'd almost fooled herself into believing she'd lost interest in him, too.

What a joke. Every time Carl came near, she fell for him all over again. It had always been that way, ever since he'd agreed to meet her for coffee so she could ask for his advice about the restaurant several years ago. Back then she'd been nervous around the millionaire, but she'd soon relaxed. Carl was a good listener. He never made her feel bad for asking a question. Instead, he took his time to explain everything to her, down to the smallest detail, treating her restaurant as if it was as important as the tech companies he'd once run.

She'd fallen for him during those conversations, and when he'd let her know he felt the same way, she'd been over the moon. She'd pressed him on whether he meant to stay in Chance Creek because what she felt for him could last a lifetime, and she couldn't start a relationship with him if he was eventually going to leave.

When he'd announced to Fila he'd found a ranch, she'd barely been able to breathe.

She'd given up on Carl—but she hadn't wanted to.

Camila picked up her pace until she was out of sight of her booth, hovering near enough to the row of portable toilets that anyone who saw her would assume she was waiting for her turn but far enough away the smell wasn't too bad. Butterflies jittered in her stomach as she prayed he wouldn't keep her waiting. Had he really found a ranch? Could she stay in the town she loved—and get the man she wanted?

"That Maya sure is nosy," Carl said when he joined her. He'd made short work of his plate of nachos in the interim, and he tossed the remains in a nearby trash can.

Camila wondered how she ever thought she could move on from him. Her whole body buzzed when he was near. He was lean from working on the Coopers' ranch every day. His muscles defined. His skin tan from being out in all weather. He was older than her but still sexy in every way. His smile and piercing blue gaze nearly undid her.

Camila was so sick of keeping her feelings to herself. Her closest friends knew about Carl, of course, but not Maya and the rest of the Turners. They'd be furious if they found out she wanted to date an honorary Cooper. Since she lived on their spread, she had to keep things under wraps—at least until she knew for sure which way her relationship with Carl was going.

"Try living with her," Camila said. "You weren't joking, about the ranch? You found—" She couldn't

even bring herself to say it, as if she could jinx something that had already happened.

"That's right."

He took one of her hands. Tugged her closer.
Looked to make sure no one was watching. "I haven't
closed on it yet, but—"

"Why not?"

"I needed you to have your say." He watched her
process his words. "I'm hoping it'll be your home, too,
someday. Camila, everything I said three years ago still
holds true."

Camila's breath caught. He'd made it clear three
years ago he was looking for something serious. That's
why she'd made her ultimatum in the first place. Now
that he was planning to buy a ranch, and letting her
know he was still interested, he'd expect her to be ready
for that serious relationship. Camila knew she was. All
her doubts and worries fell away—

Almost.

She swallowed when she thought of her parents
back in Houston.

"When can I see it?" she asked.

"Tomorrow. First thing. I've already cleared it with
the realtor," Carl said. "Meantime," he added, "everyone's going to be at the fireworks tonight. Go with me?
Seems like a good way to celebrate. It'll be dark," he
added with a grin. He lowered his voice. "I'll make sure
no Turners or Coopers see us."

"It's a date." Camila smiled despite her worries. "I'd
better get back," she told him. "Before Fila gets over-

whelmed."

"See you in a couple of hours." He gave her hand a squeeze and let her go, although Camila had a feeling he wanted to do more. She sure did. But they were in a public place, and there were Turners and Coopers everywhere. As much as she ached to touch him, run her hands over those delicious muscles, go up on tiptoe to meet his kiss—reluctantly, she tore herself away from him and said goodbye.

As she walked back to the food booth, her heart beating hard, Camila realized things were about to change. Fast. Carl wasn't looking for a fling. He'd made that clear back when they'd started all this. He wanted marriage. A family.

Which meant she needed to take care of some business of her own.

It was time to give her parents a call and clear the air between them.

Tomorrow, she decided, catching sight of the food tent, relieved not to have to think about that now. She'd be far too busy the rest of the day keeping up with her customers.

Keeping them happy was her main concern these days. The restaurant she shared with Fila was everything to her. She was proud of how professional their booth looked, with Fila's Famila emblazoned on the sign. She was proud, too, it had grown to be one of the most popular establishments in town, a real achievement after the bad start she'd made when she'd arrived here.

She'd come to Montana after fighting with her family. Back in Houston, she'd always worked in her family's restaurant, Torres de Sabores, since she was a little girl. She'd always loved cooking, and had a flair for it, but when her father made her older brother Mateo head chef, it had been the last straw after a lifetime of taking second place. Her four other brothers and two sisters had long since moved out to take other jobs. If Mateo had taken the business as seriously as she did—if he'd lived and breathed Mexican food—she'd have gladly been his second in command.

But instead, he'd taken the position as if it was owed him, spent more time chatting with customers in the front end of the restaurant than working in the back, and tried to let her carry the load—without getting any credit for it.

When it became clear to Camila nothing would change, she'd decided to strike out on her own. Although it had torn her heart in two, she'd left her family behind and come to Montana with the backing of her uncle Gerardo, who still lived in Mexico with her aunt Ximena. She'd found a building, leased a space—

And then nearly lost everything when Gerardo backed out of the deal after her father found out he was loaning her money. Thank goodness Fila had come to the rescue. Starting her own restaurant at the same time, she'd been glad for a partner, and the two of them made a stunning debut in Chance Creek. Fila's Familia was always crowded and busy. Camila was grateful for the success—and even more grateful for her first real friend in Chance Creek. She'd never forget the aching loneliness of her early days in the northern town.

She'd made a new home here. A home she loved.

But now she needed to repair the damage she'd left behind. For the past three years, it had been easy to put on hold. Her restaurant had taken up all her time, and she'd told herself she'd get to everything else when she had a spare moment. Now she wished she hadn't put it off. She had an almost superstitious pang when she thought about moving ahead with Carl before she fixed things between her and her parents.

This wasn't going to be easy. Paula expected her to move back sooner or later. She wouldn't be happy to hear Camila meant to stay in Chance Creek, and Camila had no idea how her parents would react to the idea of her becoming serious with Carl. She wanted her parents' approval of the life she'd chosen. Wanted them to love Carl as much as she did, even though he wasn't Mexican.

How would they react when they found out her plans?

Would they cut off communication with her for good?

They nearly had when she moved out. Only recently had they begun to talk more frequently by phone again. She spoke more with her brothers and sisters—except Mateo. The way she'd left had made things awkward between them.

It was time to make amends. To heal the wounds before they deepened.

She only wished she knew how.

"Something wrong?" Fila asked when Camila rejoined her and Maya at the booth.

Camila tied her apron back on and shook her head. But this was Fila—her best friend in the world. "Yes," she admitted.

"Your family?" Fila guessed.

Fila knew her too well, Camila thought ruefully.

"Maybe you should go visit them," Fila suggested. "Patch things up face-to-face."

"Maybe." She'd been thinking the same thing herself lately.

"Don't let them convince you to stay, though." Fila prepared another plate of nachos and handed it to Maya, who passed it to a customer. "We need you here."

Camila nodded. It didn't need to be a long trip. She'd apologize to her parents for upsetting them, then paint a picture of how well her life was going. And then bring up Carl...

"Three days. Four at most," Fila went on. "More than that and the whole place will come down around my ears."

Camila had to grin. "I doubt it." Fila was the most organized woman she knew. She had too strong a will to let anything overwhelm her.

"Oh, man. Here comes Uncle Jed," Maya interrupted in a low voice. "Brace yourselves."

"Maya, I've been looking for you," Jedediah Turner boomed from the other side of the counter, making Camila jump. Jed was one of the orneriest men she'd ever met, but he was her landlord, which meant she had to watch her manners around him.

"Hi, Uncle Jed," Maya said cheerfully.

"Hi, Jedidiah," Camila echoed. "How are you today?"

"I'll be fine as soon as we've won the Founders Prize." He must have once stood tall and square shouldered, but time had taken its toll. At 85, he moved stiffly, but he was as proud as ever.

"Founders Prize?" Camila exchanged a look with her friends, but they were as mystified as she was.

"Didn't you hear the big announcement? The winner will be announced on Halloween. A lot of land riding on that contest. Land that should belong to us Turners."

Camila just nodded. She wasn't a Turner, but living at the Flying W seemed to make her an honorary member of the family, which she usually appreciated. The Turners were known for being honorable, upright members of society, and for the most part, they lived up to their reputation.

Until the Coopers got involved.

Then they seemed to lose their minds.

"What land?" Maya asked.

"Settler's Ridge."

"Settler's Ridge?" Maya's eyes grew wide, and she turned to Camila to explain. "That property forms the northern boundary of the Flying W and Thorn Hill. It's on both sides of Pittance Creek. If we own it, we control the creek, right?" she asked Jed.

He nodded.

"Of course, the Coopers will want it too. What do we have to do to get it?"

"Be the biggest contributors to civic society in Chance Creek. Which we already are and always have been. It's a slam dunk," he said smugly.

Camila glanced at Maya. Was it? The Turners were good people, worked hard, went to church sometimes, participated in town events, but as far as making a contribution to civic society… didn't that require something more?

Jed must have sensed her skepticism. "We built the high school," he exclaimed.

"Back in 1953," Maya returned. "What have we donated since then?"

"How many high schools does one family have to build?" Jed answered huffily.

"It might be a case of 'What have you done for me lately,'" Fila put in.

Camila was grateful to her friend for saying so. Jed was better behaved toward outsiders than he was to Turners—real or honorary.

"Bah!" he waved a dismissive hand. "I served on the town council for forty years. I've done my bit. I'm a shoe-in for the prize."

"If you say so," Camila said slowly. She didn't like any of this. It was a set up for trouble.

Jed turned on his heel and strode off, mumbling under his breath.

"Hi, ladies. How's it going?" said Maya's sister, Stella, slipping into the booth from the back. "Sure looks busy." Twenty-seven years old with dark curls and bright hazel eyes, she scanned the customers waiting for their turn.

"We've had a lineup for most of the day," Camila told her.

"Uncle Jed's on a tear," Stella said to Maya. "I'm here to hide for a minute."

"About the Founder's Prize? He'll be pissed if someone else gets that land," Maya said. "He's pretty sure he deserves it just for being born."

"You really think the Coopers will try for it?" Camila asked.

"Jed's underestimating Virginia Cooper if he thinks they won't," Stella said. "But I don't know what we can do about it, either. It's not like we have any spare cash to donate another school." She bit her lip, caught Camila watching her and smiled. "Doesn't matter. The Coopers are worse off than we are. Still, the next six months might get messy. This might be the right time to move out—not that I want you to go," she hastened to assure Camila. "I've loved having you around the place, but didn't you say you had an appointment with Megan Lawrence about buying a house? How did that work out?"

"Not so well, but I'm going to view a place tomorrow." It wasn't technically a lie, even if she was going to view it with Carl rather than Megan. She'd gotten in touch with the realtor mostly to save face, thinking Carl had lost interest in her. She'd thought maybe if she bought her own little house in town she could hold her head up even if Carl fell for someone else.

Now she didn't have to worry about any of that.

She caught Fila's eye. "I have a really good feeling about this one."

"CARL, WOULD YOU give me a ride? I forgot something."

Carl was grateful when Olivia Cooper tugged on his sleeve an hour later. It was only six-thirty. Two hours to go before the fireworks finale to the fair, too long to wait for his first real date with Camila. He'd perused the vendor booths, ridden a couple of the carnival rides, and was just contemplating going back for another round of nachos when Olivia appeared. Blonde and full of energy, equal parts common sense and wildness, she was always a good distraction.

"Where's your truck?"

"I rode in with Lance, but he's determined to win some dumb prize at one of the game booths. He keeps plunking down change and chucking baseballs at pyramids of bottles. Waste of time and money if you ask me. So how about it? Can you drive me?"

"Sure thing." Thorn Hill was only twenty minutes away. He'd be back plenty early enough to meet Camila if they left now. Chauffeuring Olivia around would kill time.

He followed her through the crowds to the field the town had turned into a parking lot and located his deep blue Chevy Silverado in the sea of vehicles just as his phone buzzed in his pocket.

"Sven. What's up?" he asked when he took the call. Not another problem, he prayed. He didn't have time to fly to California right now.

"You won't believe it." Sven's excited tone stopped Carl in his tracks.

"What is it?"

"It's Martin Fulsom. The billionaire. One of his lawyers got in touch. He wants to buy me out!"

"Holy crap." This was big. This could make his friend rich in his own right—and could end Carl's obligation to Andersson Robotics, freeing him to concentrate fully on his life in Chance Creek.

Carl had known Sven's company was ripe for an acquisition deal—they'd structured the whole company with that idea in mind. But Fulsom was one of the biggest players around. The deal would either be spectacular—or not, if Fulsom thought he could force Sven into a weak position.

"That's the good news. The bad news is he wants to sew this up fast. If we don't get a deal done by May tenth, he's going to walk."

"Holy—crap," Carl repeated, not wanting to freak out his friend with his first choice of words. "That's a tight time frame."

"Nine days from now."

"Do you have his offer yet?"

"No. He said he'll send a written offer in a couple of days. I don't get why he's giving me a deadline when he hasn't even taken action yet."

Carl's chest tightened with concern. He'd known Fulsom by reputation for years, of course. The man regularly made headlines for his stratospheric profits and outlandish publicity events, and the television arm of his empire produced a reality TV show called *Base Camp* on a ranch right here in Chance Creek. Carl had never met the man personally, but he'd had a brush with him a while back when they'd both gone after the same ranch.

Fulsom had beaten him to the punch.

"He's trying to keep you off-balance. He'll probably use every trick in the book to make this deal go his way."

"I figured. I need you here," Sven said. "Can you fly out for a few weeks?"

Carl stifled a groan. He should have known that's why Sven had called, but his timing couldn't be worse. As always these days, he was torn between his obligation to Sven—and his desire to be here. "I've got a lot going on right now."

"Man, I need you," Sven said again. "I've never done this before."

"You'll be fine." Carl hoped he sounded surer than he felt. Fulsom was a shark—on a whole different level from anyone Sven had dealt with so far. But as much as he wanted to help his friend, he wasn't going anywhere until he'd closed on his new ranch. "You're about to be a very rich man," he added, hoping to calm Sven. "Look, I'm in the middle of something, but I'll call you first thing tomorrow morning."

"Fine," Sven said dispiritedly. Carl ended the call and tried to make small talk with Olivia as they made their way out of town, but he was distracted. Deals like this took a lot of work, and judging by his tight deadline, Fulsom meant to play hardball. Sven was right; he needed Carl's help. But Carl couldn't leave Chance Creek now. Not until he'd secured his relationship with Camila.

When they neared the turnoff to Thorn Hill, Carl put on his signal, but Olivia said, "I actually need to go to the Flying W. Noah's got something of mine. I just need to pick it up."

"Noah Turner's got something of yours?" That didn't make sense, but Carl drove onward instead of turning off, and they crossed over Pittance Creek on their way to the Flying W. "What's Noah got?"

"Just something I forgot."

Carl turned into a rutted lane, drove several hundred meters, and the Turners' house came into view. It was a large white farmhouse with a wide front porch and a green metal roof. Carl had only been here once or twice before—and he hadn't stayed long. He pulled up in front of it and parked. Olivia flung open her door and hopped out before Carl could even turn off the engine.

"I'll be back in a second!"

Carl watched her take the front steps two at a time. Instead of ringing the bell, she pulled open the screen door, grasped the knob of the front door and gave it a twist.

"Oh, hell." Carl flung open his door, too, and strode

after her. "Hey," he called. "Don't you think you should knock? Not sure Noah would appreciate us just walking in." He followed her up the steps.

"If the Turners didn't want us to walk in, they'd lock their front door." She gave it a shove, and it swung wide open.

"Is Noah here?" Carl regretted giving Olivia a ride. He should have predicted trouble when a Capulet asked for a lift to the Montague house, but he owed the Coopers a lot and didn't like to say no when they asked a favor.

"I know where it is. There's no need to bother him." Olivia slipped indoors before he could stop her. Carl hung outside, peering through the screen door, unwilling to trespass.

"Olivia. Come on," he called after her. Too late. He watched her veer to the left and enter the living room, which was all wood floors and leather sofas. He could see the head of a magnificent buck hanging on the far wall, keeping a vigil over a large stone fireplace.

He pulled the screen door open and poked his head in. "Olivia!"

"Just a second!"

Something crashed to the floor inside the house.

Hell. "What's going on in there?"

"Go!" Olivia shouted, appearing a second later. She pushed him back toward the steps, slamming the front door shut behind her, and let the screen door hit the frame with a clatter. "Go! Go! Go!" Careening past him, she stumbled on the stairs, and Carl just managed to grab her before she fell head over heels. She regained her balance, grabbed Carl's arm and dragged him toward his truck. "Start the engine," she yelled. She held something in the crook of her arm. A clock?

"What the hell, Olivia?" Carl dug in his heels to stop their headlong journey.

"Damn it, let's go!" Olivia elbowed him hard in the side, and when he folded, she yanked open the driver's side door and tried to shove him into his seat.

The house's front door burst open again, and Noah Turner appeared on the stoop. Olivia yelped and dashed around to the passenger side of Carl's truck.

"Olivia? Give it back!" Noah bellowed.

Carl froze. What the hell was going on here?

"Start the engine! Now!" Olivia yelled from inside the vehicle. "Carl, did you hear me?"

Noah clattered down the steps, crossed the driveway and tried to pull open Olivia's door. A tall, lean man with dark hair, he could look stern when he wanted to—and he obviously wanted to. He rattled the handle a few times before circling around the truck.

"Out of my way, Whitfield." Noah pushed him aside and scrambled past him into the cab of the truck.

"For fuck's sake, Turner." Carl stumbled back, caught his balance and reached for Noah.

Noah shrugged him off. "Give it to me, Olivia." He grabbed for the clock.

She wrenched it back. "It's high time it comes home where it belongs. You Turners don't need it."

"It belongs to us. I can't believe you would walk

right in and steal it!"

"I can't believe I had to!"

Losing his temper, Carl reached in and leaned on the horn. Its loud blare startled the other two.

Noah jerked back, lost his grip on the clock and hit his head on the roof of the cab. With a squeak, Olivia fell back against her door. Carl cleared his throat. "Will somebody tell me what the hell is going on?"

Olivia scrambled upright. "This clock belonged to my great-great-great granddaddy Slade Cooper," she stated. "He gave it to Ernestine Harris back in 1882 when they became engaged, to signify the time they'd spend together throughout their lives. When she dumped him and ran off with Zeke Turner instead, she kept the damn clock!" She shoved Noah. "And this reprobate's family has kept it on their damn mantel ever since. Just to piss us off!"

"You're fighting over something that happened more than a hundred and twenty years ago?" Carl had heard enough. They weren't the only ones struggling with their past—or their present. He had his own problems. Real problems. Like how to fix things in California so he could focus on Camila. "Out. Both of you."

"That's not the only thing we're fighting about," Olivia said darkly.

"Out!"

Olivia unlocked her door and got out in a huff, her ponytail swinging indignantly.

Carl walked around the truck to confront her.

"Hand it over," he demanded. "You want to steal things, do it on your own time."

Noah joined them. "I oughtta call Cab Johnson and turn you in," he said to Olivia.

"You won't turn me in. You never do." But Olivia handed over the clock.

Never do, thought Carl. How many times had Olivia tried to steal the thing?

Noah tucked it under his arm. Ducked his head. Studied his boots for a minute. "I'm heading back to the Spring Fling in a minute. Just came home to check on the cattle. I could give you a ride," he said gruffly.

"Give me a ride? That's the least you can do," she huffed. "You'd better buy me dinner, too, after the way you manhandled me."

Noah straightened to his full height. "Manhandled you? You tried to steal my family's clock."

Olivia tossed her head, and her ponytail swung. "And your family—" She glanced back at Carl and stopped midsentence. "Let's get going—I don't want to miss anything." She strode off toward Noah's truck.

To Carl's surprise, Noah's mouth quirked up into a grin. "Yes, ma'am. Let me grab my keys."

Carl watched him head back inside.

What the hell had just happened here?

"See you later, Carl. Thanks for the lift," Olivia tossed breezily over her shoulder as she climbed into Noah's Ram pickup.

"Okay," he said slowly.

A minute later, Noah returned and ran lightly down

the steps. He didn't look like a man who'd almost been robbed.

Carl watched Noah open the door to his truck and begin to climb in, but he stopped with one foot in and one foot out. "Oh, hell," he said. "Here comes trouble. Carl, you better take Olivia, after all."

Carl immediately saw why. He recognized the truck that was just pulling in. That was Liam, if he wasn't mistaken. And Jedidiah was with him. The coming confrontation wouldn't be pretty. Olivia had been breaking and entering—and now she was riding in Noah's truck.

"Olivia!" he called.

Olivia hopped out as quick as a flash and ran for Carl's vehicle, all trace of her former cockiness gone.

"What the hell's going on here?" Liam shouted, parking his truck and climbing out, a rough-and-tumble man who seemed to Carl to have something to prove to the world. "Why's that Cooper on our land?"

Carl fought not to roll his eyes. Time to diffuse the situation—fast. "I brought her here."

"And what are you doing here, city boy? Ain't no coffee houses around these parts."

That was Jedediah Turner climbing out of the passenger side, his movements slow but his speech as sharp as ever.

"Just paying a visit." Carl edged closer to his Silverado, ready to climb back in. Maybe he and Olivia could still get out of here before all hell broke loose. Olivia reached the passenger side and slipped in quickly.

Carl saw her lock the door the second it was closed.

"I doubt like hell that's the truth. You tried to steal my clock again, didn't you?" Jed pointed an accusing finger at Olivia.

Carl didn't wait for her to open her window and answer. He hopped right into the driver's seat, pulled the door shut behind him and revved the engine a second later.

"This means war!" Jed shouted after them as Carl hit the gas, peeled out and hightailed it down the lane.

For one awful moment, he thought Jed would jump back into Liam's truck and pursue them. The last thing any of them needed was a high-speed chase through town. Or for the octogenarian to have a heart attack.

"That was close," Olivia said. She didn't seem the least bit chastened by what had happened. In fact, she looked like she'd enjoyed the whole damn thing.

"Too close."

"Come on, sometimes you've got to rile things up a little, don't you think?"

Carl didn't answer that. He didn't need things riled up. He needed them to calm the heck down.

"Let's get you back to the festival" was all he said. He wasn't going to ask her about Noah. He didn't want to know. A glance at his watch told him there was still an hour to go until the fireworks.

He'd park the truck and find somewhere to hide until the time came to meet Camila—and if a Cooper or Turner got anywhere near him, he'd run like hell.

"I WISH I could have seen them hightailing it out of there," Stella Turner told Maya almost an hour later. Camila hovered as close as she could to the front of the booth, working on an order of burritos and straining to hear everything Maya's older sister said. She had raced up to the booth a few moments ago, followed by Jed, who struggled to keep up with her, leaning heavily on his cane.

Why would Carl and Olivia break into the Flying W? She had no doubt Olivia was behind it. Carl wasn't the breaking-and-entering type.

"They're lucky Liam didn't have his shotgun handy," Stella said. "He would have put out their tires. They wouldn't have gotten anywhere."

"At least we still have the clock," Maya said. "No harm, no foul, I guess."

"There's harm a-plenty where the Coopers are concerned," Jedidiah snapped. He looked as angry as a wet hen. "I told you I should move back into the house. The whole place is going to hell since I went to the damn Prairie Garden. I'm fit as a fiddle. No need for all that fussing they do there."

"Fit as a fiddle, huh? Then why was Liam taking you back to the house for a rest?" Stella asked.

"I didn't need no rest," Jed sputtered.

"You know you love all the attention from the ladies at the Prairie Garden, Uncle Jed," Maya teased. "That's why you moved there. Besides, Noah was at the house. Olivia didn't get away with it."

Camila had a feeling Maya didn't want Jed to move

back to the ranch he still nominally owned. She understood why. He would micro-manage all of them if he lived there.

"Still—"

"Come on, I want to get some ice cream before the fireworks. You said you'd treat me," Maya told Jed.

"Ice cream. At a time like this," Jed said disgustedly, but his eyes lit up, and soon all three hustled away.

"Let's pack up," Fila said to Camila. "The fireworks will start soon. I don't want to miss them."

They worked together to break down the heaviest equipment as dusk settled over them until Ned, Fila's husband, arrived in his truck with their nearly three-year-old son, Holton. Ned helped them load everything in, each of them taking turns running after the toddler when Holton made a break for it, then he and Fila said good night.

"You sure you don't want to come with us to the fireworks?" Fila asked, Holton in her arms. The little blond boy tugged her dark braid. "We're just going to park the truck again and head over."

"You three go ahead." Camila waved them on.

When she was alone, she sighed, relaxing for the first time that day as the sky darkened and the first stars appeared. If it weren't for her date with Carl, she'd probably go straight home, but when she heard a low, masculine voice behind her say, "Hey, Camila," her heart did a little flip.

"Hey, Carl." Then she remembered Stella's story. "Heard you had some excitement at the Flying W."

He looked chagrined. "That was Olivia's idea. She told me Noah had something for her. I should have known better than to believe her."

"What happened?"

Carl's story echoed Stella's. Camila couldn't help smiling. "Olivia nearly made you an accessory to a crime."

"She's lucky I was there," Carl said grimly. "Liam came gunning in hell for leather. He was looking for a fight."

Camila's good mood slipped a little. "We'd better be careful, then. After that trouble last week at the Dancing Boot, he's been pretty edgy. If anyone sees us together, it could touch off another fight."

"It's getting dark. We'll go grab a place on the lawn. Somewhere shadowy."

"Sounds good."

They dropped off the rest of the supplies at her truck, and Carl took her hand as he led her toward the field where people were sitting to wait for the fireworks. His large hand engulfed her small one, and as usual, she was aware of Carl's strength. There was something so masculine about him. Something that always made her want to touch him when he was near.

He surveyed the wide lawn, and Camila knew what he was thinking. There wasn't exactly anywhere shadowy here. Carl led her to the far side of the crowd.

"I guess I should have brought a blanket," he said, nodding at the other couples and families spread out on the lawn.

"That's okay." Camila wasn't dressed up; she didn't care if her jean shorts got grass stains. She was only concerned about getting caught.

Which was ridiculous when she thought about it. She and Carl shouldn't have to worry about what the Turners and Coopers got up to. She decided she'd enjoy her time with Carl. Soon she wouldn't have to worry about the Turners anymore. When she left the Flying W, she wouldn't owe them anything.

They found a spot and sat down. Carl heaved a sigh as he settled in. "Feels like I'm always running these days," he said, plucking a blade of grass and twirling it in his fingers.

"Know what you mean."

He tossed the blade of grass away and touched her arm. "I'm glad to be here with you, though. I've been waiting a long time for this."

"To watch fireworks?" she teased.

"To watch fireworks," he confirmed. "And to do this."

He leaned over, and Camila sucked in a breath, closed her eyes and waited for his kiss. She'd fantasized about this moment a million times, but if she was honest, she'd stopped believing it would ever happen. Now here they were here, and—

Carl swore. "Watch out. We've got company." He pulled back, leaving Camila to open her eyes again. Heat flared up her cheeks. She must have looked ridiculous waiting there for him to plant one on her.

Carl quickly shifted a few feet away from her. Camila turned and saw Maya wending her way through the crowd. Maya waved cheerfully. "Hi!" she called out.

Camila's heart sank. She glanced at Carl, but he was looking in the other direction, as if he hadn't been milliseconds from kissing her.

A moment later Maya plunked herself down beside Camila, balancing an ice cream cone in one hand and holding the blanket in the other. "There you are. I was looking for you." She tossed a blanket over Camila's legs. "Whoops! Stand up a minute, would you, and I'll spread this out."

Camila did as she was told and sent an apologetic glance to Carl behind Maya's back. He shrugged. She knew what he meant; what could they do?

"Uh, Maya—" she began, still hoping for a chance to be alone with him.

"Hey, great—this is a terrific spot to see the fireworks," Stella called out, hurrying toward them. She plopped herself down on the blanket Maya had spread. "Liam, over here!" she shouted and waved at her brother. To Camila's horror, Liam waved back and began to thread through the crowd toward them, too. A moment later Noah joined him, leading Jed by the elbow.

Camila bit back a long-suffering sigh. Had she really thought she and Carl could find privacy in this crowd? That's not how things worked here in Chance Creek.

"I don't need no help," Jed was saying as he leaned heavily on his cane and lowered himself onto the large blanket. "Don't know why I bothered coming. Seen more fireworks than I can count in my lifetime."

"And you always enjoy them, Uncle Jed," Stella told him. "Here's your ice cream." She handed him a sundae. "Besides, you wouldn't want to be inside on a beautiful night like this."

Jed made a rude noise, and despite her frustration, Camila bit back a laugh. Sometimes being around the Turners made her feel better about her own family.

Still, she turned a chagrined glance toward Carl, who was pretending to be engrossed in his cell phone. He caught her eye and winked. "It's okay," he mouthed at her. "Later."

She nodded—and saw Liam take notice of Carl's proximity, then stiffen.

"Hey, Whitfield; don't you belong on the Cooper side of the crowd?"

"Not exactly a lot of places to sit," Carl told him and didn't budge despite Liam's belligerent tone. Instead he lifted a hand to wave at Lance Cooper. "Hey, Lance! Over here," he called.

Camila could have kicked him. Didn't he know he was playing with fire?

Was he doing it on purpose?

He was, damn him. She supposed she couldn't fault him for it; she'd let Maya sit with her. But how could she have stopped the woman? Now Maya and the rest of the Turners were frowning as Lance approached.

Lance was thirty-two, with dark hair and gray eyes. Camila didn't know him well, but she imagined Carl worked with the man on a daily basis at Thorn Hill.

Lance dropped down on the grass near Carl, only then seeming to notice the cluster of Turners on the blanket with Camila.

He turned his back to them. "Hi, Carl."

"Hi, Lance," Carl said. "How goes it?"

"Good enough. Until now," he added loudly enough for all of them to hear. Camila shook her head when Carl caught her eye, then jumped when Lance suddenly yelled, "Steel! Over here."

Camila felt Maya and Stella straightening by her side. Steel Cooper was a notorious troublemaker, although Camila couldn't say what kind of trouble he made. There were rumors of fights—and more. Maybe jail time. Steel's hair was as dark as Lance's. There was stubble on his chin, his eyes sharp and gray. He looked like a fighter, Camila thought.

Following close behind him was his sister Olivia, blond hair pulled back in a ponytail. They made their way over and sat down next to Lance. Camila felt like a rabbit among foxes as the Coopers and Turners eyed one another sideways.

"Humph!" Camila looked up to see old Virginia Cooper marching their way. "What is this, Armistice Day?"

"There wasn't anywhere else to sit," Lance said petulantly.

"Life is never through offering its indignities," Virginia pronounced, but she put out a hand and allowed Steel to help her lower to the ground. She sat ramrod straight and never looked at Jedidiah. But Jed was looking at Virginia.

Interesting, Camila thought as the first firecracker exploded into the air. Then she noticed Carl watching her, too, and found it hard to think at all.

Chapter Two

C ARL PICKED UP Camila at the restaurant the following morning, where they'd agreed to meet to go see Hilltop Acres. The sunshine and warm temperatures lifted Carl's spirits, and he kept the windows open to let the breeze cool them.

"That was kind of like watching fireworks in the DMZ last night," Camila said when she got into his truck.

Carl chuckled. "Yeah, it was a little tense. I'd hoped we'd get a chance to be alone."

"Me, too. But we're alone now."

Carl took her hand and held it as he drove, content for the first time in weeks. He'd buy the ranch; they'd start to date and finally take a step toward a shared future.

But as the minutes ticked by, he noticed Camila frown.

"This place is a little far out of town," he admitted. Camila worked restaurant hours, which left her driving home late at night. The commute would be inconvenient in the winter. He hadn't thought about that yesterday.

Camila chewed her lip. "A little."

Carl's shoulders tensed, and he let go of her hand as he guided the truck through a sharp turn. If she said no to this ranch, how many more years would he have to wait? The miles slipped away, and now that he knew Camila was worried about the distance, he worried about it, too. It seemed like ages before he caught sight of the turnoff to Hilltop Acres.

"Here it is." His relief was reflected on Camila's face. Good—she wanted this to work as much as he did.

He navigated the dirt track that led up an incline, parked his truck outside the vacant, timber-framed home, climbed out and stretched to unkink his back. "I know it's rough, but if I make an offer today, it's ours."

Carl gave Camila a condensed version of the tour Megan had given him the day before. Hilltop Acres would support a small herd of cattle, but he knew Camila wasn't as interested in that side of things.

"I couldn't get Megan up here this early to open the place," he told her as she stared at the small house. "We'd tear this down and rebuild it anyway."

"That's great," she finally said, and he could tell she was trying to be enthusiastic. "It's just... far from work."

"I know. It's not my dream ranch, either. But—" He lifted his hands. This was their only choice. Unless he took Virginia up on her offer.

Camila nodded slowly. "It's the only one around, huh?"

CORA SETON

"I've been looking—hard. I never stopped. You need to know that, Camila," he told her. "I think we can make this work, and if something better comes along— we'll grab it, if we can. I don't want to wait anymore. Do you?"

"No." She surveyed the house again and squared her shoulders. "Like you said, we'll make the best of it and maybe someday…" She shrugged.

He met her gaze. "You're giving me the go-ahead to make an offer?"

"It's your house, Carl. You should do what you think is right."

"I want it to be our house. Soon. Understand?" She had to know it was why he was doing this. If it wasn't for her ultimatum, he'd be holding out for a real spread. One of the bigger ones. He was a *go big or go home* kind of guy. Hilltop Acres was barely big enough to be respectable.

"I understand. I don't want you to make a mistake."

"If you like it, it won't be." He saw her frown. "I'm not asking you to commit to the ranch forever; just for now. If things go that way between us," he added for form's sake. Had he misunderstood her all this time? They'd talked about what he wanted three years ago. He didn't just want to date Camila. He wanted to marry her. Nothing had changed his mind in all that time.

Camila nodded slowly. "I do like it. But I'm not going to tell you what to do. I can't, Carl."

He tamped down his frustration. He guessed he couldn't blame her. They hadn't gone on a single date in three years. She'd thought he'd given up on them. Of course she didn't want to jump the gun.

"Come here." He held out a hand. At least they were alone. Time for that kiss he'd missed out on last night. His body came awake at the idea. God, he'd waited far too long. "I'm sorry I made you wait."

Camila nodded. Took his hand. Allowed him to pull her close. Went up on tiptoe—

"Hello!" a woman called out. "Are you the owners?"

Carl stepped back, and Camila lost her balance. He grabbed her arm to steady her. Let go again almost as fast, afraid it was a Cooper or Turner. Hell, he needed to get a hold of himself.

"No. Not yet, anyway," he called back with feigned cheerfulness as a young couple approached. He saw their truck parked down the lane. He hadn't even heard them pull in.

"Uh-oh. Competition," the man said. They were in their early thirties, Carl guessed.

"We just saw the listing last night," the woman said. "We had to see it."

"I'm planning to make an offer," Carl told her.

"Well, we'll look around. Just in case," the man added. They moved off toward the house.

"I'm late," Camila said softly. "We'd better head back to town."

"I'll drive straight to the realtor's and get this deal done," Carl promised her as they hurried back to his Silverado.

It took all his attention to negotiate the winding

road back to town. He was pushing the speed limit—a little. He needed to put in his offer before that couple decided they were interested, too. He dropped off Camila at the restaurant and was about to pull out of his parking space when his phone buzzed. It was Megan on the line. Carl parked again and took the call.

"I was about to come see you," he said. "I'm ready—"

"Listen, Carl—"

"Me, first," he interrupted. "Camila said yes. She liked Hilltop Acres. We'll take it."

Megan was quiet so long he thought she might have hung up.

"Megan?"

"That's what I called to tell you, Carl. The ranch sold last night."

FILA WAS LATE, too, this morning, and Camila decided to use the time alone to call her folks. If Carl was buying the ranch they'd just seen, then her life was about to change. She needed to make sure she sorted out her problems with her parents before too much time passed.

"Bueno," her mother, Paula, answered when she picked up.

"Hi, Mom."

"Mija? When are you coming home?"

"Por Dios." Camila took a calming breath. "Actually, I'm—"

"It's your father's birthday in five days. You weren't

here last year. You must come!"

"That's what I'm trying to tell—"

"You should make time for your family. Who knows how long we'll be here on this earth."

"Mamá—"

"Don't argue with me." Her mother's heavy accent reminded Camila of her childhood. With five brothers and two sisters, the small house had always been a noisy, chaotic place. Camila missed those days. But she didn't miss these conversations.

"You've never been here to visit me," she pointed out.

Her mother expelled a breath. "We have a restaurant, *mija*. It's hard to get away."

Was she serious? "I have a restaurant, too, Mom. Did you forget?"

"Ay. What is it you call that food you cook? *Fusion* food?"

Her tone took Camila aback, and she counted to ten. "Yeah, that's what I call it." Her parents had been furious when she left Houston, but their animosity toward her restaurant always took her by surprise. They hadn't wanted her to head up the kitchen in Houston. Why were they so bitter about the establishment she'd opened here?

Camila was proud of the way she and Fila had combined their families' cuisines to create something new, and their customers were thrilled with the results. Wasn't that what America was? A melting pot? Their Afghan-Mexican dishes were a hit. Her family refused to hear that, though.

"Come down here, and I'll show you how to really cook."

"You want me to come home for a cooking lesson?" This really took the cake, even for her mother, but Paula's sigh made her swallow the angry words she meant to say.

"Are you ever coming home again or not?"

"That's why I'm calling," she finally managed to say. "I do want to come home for *Papá*'s birthday. And… I've been seeing this guy," she added. That was true. Even if she hadn't been dating Carl, she had been seeing him around town.

Her mother's tone grew suspicious. "How long?"

"Three years." Technically true.

Paula grunted. "Why have I never heard of this man?"

Camila ignored the question. Her mother knew the answer to it already. "We're getting pretty serious, and even though nothing is set yet, I just want—" She took a deep breath and steeled herself. "I want to make sure that if he does propose at some point, I have your blessing to say yes."

Her mother didn't answer, and Camila wondered if she'd managed to surprise her. After all, she'd never mentioned Carl before, and after running off, maybe her mother hadn't thought she'd follow the old custom. Camila knew most Americans didn't bother consulting their parents about such things, but a good Mexican girl wanted her parents' permission. Camila couldn't bear it if being with Carl drove an even deeper wedge between her and her family.

"If you want my blessing," Paula finally answered stiffly, "I'll have to meet the man." Before Camila could protest, she added, "And then there's your father. He is far more stubborn. So, see? Now, you have to come home. And bring this man with you. The sooner the better." Her mother hesitated. "In fact, come today."

"Today?" Camila gripped the phone. She couldn't possibly come today.

"Today," her mother confirmed. "I have a special present in mind for your father. You know he has been very low, and this will pick him up."

"Low?" Guilt sparked inside her. Sometimes her father had moods, and it was hard to raise his spirits. She lived so far away she wasn't any help with that.

"*Mija*, he is getting old. We both are. We miss our home."

"Of course." She knew that, too. But she didn't understand why her parents didn't move back to Mexico if they missed it so badly. Their children were grown and doing fine for themselves. Surely, they could retire.

Her parents didn't talk about money, though. Not with her.

"What can I do to help?" she asked.

"Come here to Houston. Tonight. It will take a couple of days to get his gift."

Camila knew better than to argue. Her mother had been trying to get her to come home for months, and now she had found a way to force the issue.

"I'll call when I've booked my flights," she assured her mother before hanging up. As soon as Fila came in, they could figure out how to cover her shifts while she was gone. She doubted Carl would be able to come with her on such short notice.

But she'd ask.

WHEN CARL SAW Camila's name on the screen of his phone, he forced himself to stop pacing the floor of his tiny cabin, where he'd retreated as soon as Megan had given him the bad news. He'd searched the MLS ranch listings again and ordered her to do the same. "We need to find something even better. Today," he'd barked at her.

"I'll do my best."

But Carl knew it was useless. There wasn't anything better than Hilltop Acres. There wasn't anything at all—not in Chance Creek. If they'd been willing to move farther away, there would be plenty of choices, but that wasn't an option when Camila owned a business in town. He didn't know how he'd tell her, either. She'd been so happy on the way back from viewing the place.

It was as if the town itself was rejecting him—making it impossible to settle down and win Camila's heart. As if the land itself was telling him he wasn't worthy to be a Montana rancher. That galled him. Hadn't he put in his time? Put his shoulder to the wheel and spent hours learning this new work? He never did anything by half measures. He'd paid his dues.

Apparently that wasn't good enough.

Virginia popped into his mind.

Was that ranch she'd mentioned real?

Maybe it was time to find out.

"Hey, Camila," he said when he took the call, trying to keep his tone level. "How's work?" He was determined to fix this somehow before she ever found out.

"Fine," Camila said, but she sounded tense, too. Carl's neck muscles tightened. Had she heard the news about the ranch somehow? "So, this is a little crazy," she went on, "but my parents want to meet you. I don't suppose you could make it out to Houston in the next few days?"

Carl tried to conceal his relief. Meet her parents? Sure thing. That was easy compared to confessing what had happened. "Of course I can."

"You'll come?" Camila sounded relieved. "Thanks. It really means a lot to me."

"No problem," he said. "I'm serious about us. I want to go the distance, and meeting your parents is a big part of that." He made himself chuckle. "Buying a ranch, meeting the family—maybe one of these days we'll even go on a real date."

Camila laughed, too. "I'd like that. I'm going to fly to Houston tonight, if you want to come with me."

"I'd love to," Carl said, "but there's… something I have to take care of first. Can I join you tomorrow?"

"Sure. It is pretty short notice." But he could tell she was disappointed.

"I'll catch up as soon as I can," he promised her.

"I'll text the details," she told him.

When she was gone, Carl called Virginia.

"I'm in," he said without preamble. "When can we meet?"

"Right now. I'm at the house with Olivia." She sounded far too pleased by this development.

"I'll be right over."

Fifteen minutes later they were seated in the Coopers' large brick farmhouse's living room, and Olivia had headed into town. Carl had always liked it here. With its wide-plank floors mellowed by time and its heavy, sturdy furniture, it was a room that could hold several dozen people but still felt intimate, too.

"We need the proposal done by May twelfth," Virginia was saying. "That's the last day the school board can vote on new projects."

"That's not much time to get it right," Carl said. Especially if he was going to spend the next few days in Houston.

Virginia shrugged. "I don't make the rules. That's the cutoff for approving any projects the school board wants to undertake this summer. We have to get it done before then, and we need a top-notch presentation, ASAP. I've notified the architect of your ideas. You'll need to coordinate—"

"Architect?" Carl repeated. "You already hired an architect?"

"He's tackled the obvious problems with the high school, but he doesn't know what you need for the robotics department."

"Wait. Hold up. You stood there yesterday and

asked me for ideas like you didn't know where to start."

"And you came up with a doozy, just as I'd hoped," Virginia said smoothly. "You should be proud of yourself."

Carl struggled for composure. Had Virginia outfoxed him? She was the one who'd mentioned the high school.

He'd been played.

He must be getting rusty.

"Can you get the proposal done?" she pressed.

"If I do, you'll give me the inside scoop on this ranch?"

"If our proposal is approved," she confirmed.

"It'll be approved," he said wearily and left as soon as he could.

Carl returned to his cabin and drew out his phone. He had to work fast if he was flying to Houston tomorrow. He didn't want Camila to know what he was doing—both because he was aiding a Cooper to trump the Turners and because he didn't want her to know he was scrambling to get a chance to bid on another ranch. He still couldn't believe he'd lost Hilltop Acres.

But he had—and now he was paying the price.

As he called Sven, he wished he'd been more helpful last time they'd talked. It would serve him right if his friend hung up on him.

"Carl, just the man I need!" Sven said cheerfully when he picked up.

"Hey, Sven. Got a minute?"

"Of course. I've been waiting for you to call."

Heck, this was bad. He'd forgotten his promise to get in touch earlier. Carl braced himself. Time to lay his cards on the table. "Look, I know you're worried about the Fulsom deal, but I've got a problem, too. You know I want to settle here in Chance Creek, right?"

"Yeah." Sven sounded impatient, and Carl didn't blame him. He was probably dying to talk about Fulsom.

"I've finally got a line on a ranch." He'd told Sven all about Camila over the years. In fact, Sven liked to send him real estate listings from around the world. All the ranches up for sale—everywhere but Chance Creek. "Thing is, I have to do something before I can get it."

"Do what?"

"Renovate a school—and more. Here's what I have in mind." He explained the project as thoroughly as he could. When he was done, Sven was quiet.

"Well—you're always telling me I need more practice negotiating, so here goes," he finally said. "I'll put together a sponsorship package for your school—including the money, the specs for building a robotics program and a pledge for ongoing support—if you come out here and stay until I've cut my deal with Fulsom."

It was Carl's turn to be quiet. "No can do," he said finally. "I'm meeting Camila and her family in Houston tomorrow, and I'm not sure how long I'll be there. Counteroffer: I come out to help you the last two days before you finalize the deal."

"Three days," Sven said.

"Two days, and I'll work with you over email in the meantime."

"And you'll call me once a day until then?"

"Done." Camila couldn't fault him for talking to an old friend on the phone in the evenings.

"Okay, then," Sven said. "Let's get down to business."

"I JUST GOT to Houston. Now you want me to go to Mexico?"

Camila sat in the kitchen of her childhood home early the next morning, thinking it looked like she'd never left, with its cheerful yellow curtains at the window and the same plastic placemats on the table she remembered from years ago. Her mother, however, had aged. So had her father, from what little she'd seen of him. He'd accepted a peck on the cheek when she'd come in last night, then sat down to watch a soccer game on television after only a few awkward exchanges. This morning he was already at the family's restaurant helping prepare for the day with her brother.

Mateo still lived at home with her parents. One of Camila's sisters, Lupe, lived in the suburbs now, married to a man she'd met at Texas State. She worked as a physical therapist. Her other sister, Silvia, owned a flower shop. Her brothers lived in condos downtown. Marco was an accountant with an up-and-coming firm. Miguel had joined the police force, and they'd already made him a detective. Her youngest brothers, Javier and Roberto, were both auto mechanics.

She'd seen Mateo only briefly this morning before he left for the restaurant.

"Some people get to take it easy, huh?" was all he'd said as he'd rushed around the kitchen, then headed out the door.

Camila didn't bother to tell him about all her early mornings. She and Fila each worked five days a week and ran their restaurant with little help. Bess Warner was a young mother who worked the till, and Melanie Roberts was a seasoned cook who filled in on the days one of them took off. Otherwise, she and Fila did it all.

"What's wrong with Mexico?" her mother demanded.

"I've never been!"

"Exactly. How can you call yourself a Mexican chef if you've never even been there?"

Camila couldn't answer that. She wasn't the one who'd refused to cross the border. Her mother's stubbornness had kept them on the American side throughout her childhood, and she'd been too busy—and too poor—since she'd left for Montana to take a vacation.

But that wasn't why her cheeks warmed when Paula asked her question.

Camila was glad none of her friends from Montana were here to witness this conversation. Maybe none of them would even remember the lie she'd told when she first moved to Chance Creek. But she did.

Why, oh why had she concocted a fake background when none of them would even care?

Because she'd been afraid they'd feel the same way her mother did—that she couldn't possibly run a Mexican restaurant—or even an Afghan-Mexican fusion restaurant—if she wasn't from Mexico.

The truth was she was born in the United States, as were four of her brothers and both sisters. Only Mateo was born in Guerrero. When she'd left Houston to forge her own way, still stinging from the injustice of not being allowed to head up the kitchen in her family's restaurant because she was a woman, she'd vowed to prove she was just as good as Mateo. But when she reached Chance Creek and nearly went broke trying to open her restaurant, she'd been scared and alone after her uncle reneged on his promise to help fund her. When she learned a young woman was opening a restaurant next door—a woman who seemed to have the backing of half the town—Camila had panicked.

And lied.

"I'm from Mexico," she'd said, playing up her normally slight accent, pronouncing it "Mehico," which even her father had given up years ago. "I lived there until I was sixteen. I'm going to open an authentic Mexican restaurant."

Thank God Fila had become her friend, and they'd joined forces.

Thank God no one seemed to remember her stupid lie these days.

Except her.

"What am I supposed to do when I get there?" she asked her mother. When Paula had said she needed help with a gift, Camila had assumed it was something they could buy in Houston. Instead her mother was sending her across the border. Camila wanted to know why.

"Visit your family." Paula kept busy whipping up a batch of tortillas. Camila itched to help her but was afraid if she did her mother would criticize her technique. Considering Camila made hundreds of them a day for her own restaurant, she didn't think she could take that.

She shoved her hands in her pockets and waited for her mother to continue. There was something going on here, and Camila wished her mother would simply come right out and say what she really wanted.

"Whatever you're sending me to do must be pretty shady if you can't even say it out loud."

It was a shot in the dark, but her arrow hit home. Her mother's brow furrowed, and she slapped the tortilla she was shaping on the press harder than necessary. "It's not shady. The mask belongs to your father, not Aunt Ximena."

"Mask?" Now they were getting somewhere. "That wouldn't be the Olmec mask you're talking about?" If it was, this wasn't just an errand—it was the start of an international incident. That ceremonial jade mask had been passed down in her family for generations, if stories were to be believed, and was rumored to have once been part of the household of the last Aztec emperor, Cuauhtemoc. Which had to be wildly inaccurate; the mask was old, but she doubted it was that old.

Still, her parents felt the mask was a very important

part of their heritage. They'd never sell it, so this wasn't about money.

Why did her mother want it so badly?

"Is *Tía* Ximena giving it to him for his birthday?"

"It's not for her to give!" Her mother pulled the lever of the press and flattened the ball of maize flour mixed with water and salt into a small circle. She peeled it off the press, scooped up another ball of the soft dough, rolled it between her palms and put it on the press.

"Let me get this straight." Camila's temper was rising. "You want me to fly to Mexico and steal it? And then sneak it over the border? *Bueno, Mamá*. Sounds like fun."

Her mother yanked the handle of the press down forcefully. "It belongs to your father. You just go there, ask for it and bring it back. No big deal."

"Then why don't you do it?"

"You know why I won't do it."

"No, I don't." She was beginning to wish she'd never come.

"Do you wish to break my heart?" Her mother slapped another ball of dough on the press. "When I crossed the border to this country, I swore I'd never return until I was going home for good. I'm still here."

Not this again. "*Mamá*—"

"*Matriarca* of the family. That's what Ximena called herself—straight to your father's face!"

Camila didn't believe that. For one thing, her father hadn't seen his sister in years.

"Over the phone," her mother clarified. "Straight to his face! As if our moving to Texas changes anything."

Camila sighed. She knew her mother and Ximena had their differences. Camila had heard so much about her aunt and uncle over the years, she felt she knew them. But the truth was she didn't. She'd never seen them in person.

Or any of her cousins. There was Arturo and Luis—and Juana. Camila rolled her eyes. Juana the perfect daughter. Despite her mother's bickering with Ximena, her father spoke fondly of all three of them—but held his niece in especially high esteem.

When Camila was a child, she'd dreamed her cousin would come to Houston and they'd be like sisters. They were only months apart in age, whereas her own sisters were older and had always been closer to each other than they were to her. Whenever she was lonely or her feelings had been hurt, she'd tell herself stories of the way Juana would come to her rescue.

But as she grew up, and Juana did, too, her aunt's letters sung her daughter's praises so highly Camila had become jealous of her cousin, especially when her father waved those letters in her face and told her he wished he had a daughter like that. A real Mexican daughter— not the kind of girl who used American slang and sassed her parents.

During a particularly rebellious phase, she'd gathered some of those letters and set them on fire in the brick outdoor fireplace in their backyard. Oh, she'd gotten in trouble then, and Juana had soared to new heights as a paragon in her father's eyes.

Now Camila could almost see the humor in it all.

Almost.

She'd seen photos of her cousin, and Juana still out-classed her by far. Slim, with sleek long hair and a perpetually serene expression in her pictures, she was a far cry from Camila's curves and thick, bouncy, wavy curls. Camila could rarely corral her wild hair into any kind of order. She was sure not a lock of Juana's tresses ever dared to rebel.

And no one would ask Juana to cross the border and steal an heirloom. "*Mamá*, I wish I could help but—"

Her mother slapped a tortilla onto the growing pile.

"Go to Mexico. Get the mask. Bring it back. Then I will give you my blessing to be with this Carl."

Was that a threat? "And if I don't?"

Paula shrugged expressively. "Who is this gringo who wants to be with my daughter? Why should I entrust him with my child?"

"That's blackmail."

Paula shrugged again.

"Have you told them I'm coming, at least?"

Her mother was indignant. "*Por supuesto*. What do you think I am?"

"I don't know," Camila mumbled.

"I heard that." Her mother looked skyward. "*Ay, Dios,* I hope they like you. If I was a good mother, you will remember how to behave, even after so long in *Montaña*. I fear I failed you, and you'll give the wrong impression."

"In other words, don't screw up," Camila said flatly.

"The mouth on you!" Paula swatted her.

"Don't worry. I'll make sure to be very polite when I steal our closest relatives' most precious possession.

Maybe if I behave myself, I won't even wind up in jail. I'm going to go pack my things."

She headed to her childhood room, shut the door and plunked herself down on her old bed. Carl had texted her his itinerary, and he was due any minute, so she decided to break the news about her junket to Mexico when he arrived. At least he'd get to meet her mother before she flew out. Maybe she could take him to the restaurant quickly to meet her father, too. She expected Carl would fly straight back home afterward, and she wished she could have saved him the trip. Carl was a busy man. She hated to think she'd wasted his time, especially when her mother had made it clear she'd withhold her blessing until that stupid mask was in her hands.

To pass the time she texted Fila. It was early enough Fila would just be getting started at the restaurant.

Might be away longer than expected.

An answer came swiftly. *Why? You okay?*

I'm fine, Camila answered. *But I'm going to Mexico.*

MEXICO???

Camila laughed when Fila followed up with, *You'd better come back.*

I'm coming back. She wished she was back in Chance Creek right now.

A text from Maya Turner popped up. *Hey, where are you?*

Whoops. Camila had been in such a hurry she'd forgotten to notify the Turners she was leaving. *Houston. Visiting family,* she replied just as a text from Fila came in: *How are your folks? Made any progress?*

Not really, she texted back. Not until she got that mask.

You heard about Liam and Lance? texted Maya.

Are you sure you're coming back? A text from Fila popped up, too.

Camila replied to Maya first. *What now?*

She flipped back to Fila, but a reply from Maya appeared right away. *Got into a race—on the road out to the ranches. The sheriff is furious—he caught them at it. Took both of their licenses for ten days. Boy, is Liam pissed.*

That sounds bad, Camila wrote. She wished the feud would just go away. *Be back as soon as I can,* she answered Fila.

Rumor has it Carl Whitfield's helping the Coopers try to win the prize. If they've got a millionaire on their side, we're hooped, Maya texted.

We're not hooped, Camila wrote. The way rumors flitted around Chance Creek, it was no wonder people got in fights. Too late she realized she'd sent the text to Fila.

Of course we're not hooped. Who says we're hooped? Fila replied.

Camila sighed.

That wasn't meant for you. I'll text you later, okay?

She told Maya she'd get back to her later, too, then turned off her phone. Carl wasn't helping the Coopers with anything. He was on his way here.

To meet her family.

Chapter Three

CARL HESITATED ON the Torres' front stoop, wondering what his reception would be when he entered Camila's family's house. Normally, introductions didn't intimidate him, but he'd never gone to meet the parents of a woman he wanted to marry before. He'd been engaged years ago to a woman named Lacey Taylor, but she'd been estranged from her family, and she'd broken off the relationship and moved to Billings. When he thought back on it, Carl could only shake his head. He'd had no idea what he was doing back then. So high off making his millions he hadn't looked past a pretty face and a cute country accent to see that he and Lacey had nothing in common.

Thank God she'd come to her senses or he might be miserable right now.

Camila was nothing like Lacey.

And he had nothing to fear from her parents, he told himself. He was a man of substance. He could be proud of his accomplishments. He loved the Torres' daughter. What more could they want?

It was still early in the morning, the street relatively quiet. This was a respectable neighborhood with small, tidy houses. He imagined that most people were just getting up. An older man was tending to a bed of flowers a few houses down. The scrape of his trowel carried on the still air.

The Torres' door swung open before he could knock.

"Carl."

Camila took his breath away every time he saw her. She was so alive. So warm and compassionate. Her laugh infectious…

She wasn't laughing now, though. In fact, she was frowning.

"Everything all right?" he asked her.

She gave a small smile. "Just fine," she said. "Except I have to take a trip to Mexico—and I'm leaving as soon as I can."

"Mexico?"

"You'd better come in and sit down. Carl—" Camila broke off, bit her lip, then lowered her voice. "My family is pretty conservative, so… behave yourself, okay?"

He didn't get to ask what that meant. An older woman with a stern expression joined Camila in the doorway, her hair coiled into a severe bun.

"Carl, this is my mother, Paula Torres. Mom, this is Carl Whitfield."

"Nice to meet you," Carl said.

Paula looked him up and down, nodded once and turned to usher him inside. "My daughter is going to Mexico to fetch her father's present."

"Present?"

"It's a long story." Camila led the way into the living room, and they all took seats. "My family owns this jade mask. It's been handed down from generation to generation, and now it belongs to my father. But when he came to America, he left it behind in the safekeeping of his sister, thinking he'd only be gone for a few years. Since he's still here after all this time, my mother thinks it's time to go get it."

As Camila continued to fill him in, Carl took in her mother's emphatic nods and the righteous lift of her chin, and understood. Paula had somehow been as crafty as Virginia. Anyone could tell Camila didn't want to go to Mexico. He wondered how Paula had forced her hand.

Now he and Camila would be apart again. Unless…

"I'm coming with you," he interrupted Camila. "To Mexico."

CAMILA KNEW SHE must be gaping at Carl. "But… you're so busy—"

"Doesn't matter." He turned to her mother. "Can you let your sister-in-law know to expect me, too?"

Paula pursed her lips, then nodded reluctantly, and Camila knew she wasn't happy about Carl's interference, but she had the feeling that as much as Paula resented his high-handedness, Carl had gone up in her estimation. "I will tell her." She seemed to remember her manners. "Can I bring you something to drink?"

"Just water would be great."

"Camila, fetch Mr. Whitfield some water," her mother ordered, preventing any chance for the two of them to be alone. Camila wanted to tell him he didn't have to come. And he didn't have to answer her mother's questions, either. She didn't want him mixed up in her family's crazy affairs. But she did as her mother said, and when she returned, she found her mother well into an interrogation.

"I understand you intend to marry Camila."

Camila's breath whooshed out of her and she collapsed onto the sofa, nearly spilling the water she'd fetched before Carl reached over and took it. She'd made it clear she and Carl hadn't gotten that far, but her mother was getting back at him—and her.

Carl gave Camila a look that made her heart squeeze, then turned back to her mother. "I do," he said seriously. "I hope that's not why you wanted to send her to Mexico—to keep her away from me."

Camila had to hand it to him. He was playing her mother perfectly.

Paula demurred. She couldn't be rude straight to his face, even if he had riled her. She was far too well-mannered for that. Carl had better watch out, though. "The mask is a family heirloom. You value family, do you not, Mr. Whitfield?"

"Carl," he told her. "And of course I do. Family is very important."

"So is heritage. Something Camila must learn."

Carl frowned. "I understand." But his tone made it clear he didn't.

"My husband's birthday is in four days." Paula folded her hands in her lap.

"Which is why I have to leave today," Camila rushed to tell Carl. She didn't want him to think she was the one pushing all of this. "It might take me a few days to—" she couldn't tell him she was going to steal it "—get it. I need to be back for the party."

"That's fine."

"Are you sure?" She couldn't believe he wanted to come.

"I'm sure. Mexico is dangerous, you know. You shouldn't travel alone." He met Paula's gaze and held it. To Camila's surprise, her mother was the first to look away. But then she looked back again. Glanced at Carl's expensive watch. Looked him up and down.

Camila could almost see the wheels turning. She hoped Carl wasn't catching the calculations clearly spinning in her mother's head—but she had a feeling he was.

"Muy bien." Paula stood up and clapped her hands together, suddenly all business. "I shall call Ximena. You—book the flights," she ordered Carl as she passed. "You should leave within the hour."

"Mamá," Camila protested. "Carl just got here—"

It was no use. Paula bustled to the kitchen to call her sister-in-law and tell Ximena to expect another guest, leaving Camila with a desire to run and hide.

"I'm so sorry for all of this," she told Carl as he pulled out his cell phone and started looking for a flight. "You don't have to come. You know that, don't you?"

He smiled, and mischief lit his eyes. "And miss a chance to take a vacation to Mexico with my girlfriend?"

His girlfriend? Camila liked the sound of that, and she hoped this wouldn't all blow up in her face. She wished they truly were taking a vacation—without all the complications her family was adding to the equation.

She'd been stupid, hadn't she? Setting up rules that had kept them apart. Especially such dramatic ones. She could have believed him when he said he meant to make Chance Creek his home. Why had she forced the issue—demanded he buy a ranch?

A glance around her family home reminded her why. Everything here touched on memories that were special to her. Despite her differences with her family, she had loved growing up here, and leaving her home had been heart-wrenching. When she'd settled in Chance Creek, she'd created a new home and a new family made up of friends who'd grown dear to her. She'd made a promise to herself she'd never leave again. Before she could give her heart to a man, she needed proof he felt the same way.

And here Carl was, willing to give that to her.

He was buying a ranch, for heaven's sake. Maybe the Hilltop Acres wasn't perfect, but they'd have a home in Chance Creek no one could take away from them.

"You really don't have to come," she repeated. Did he wonder if she'd always be like this—bossing him around, and demanding houses and trips to foreign countries?

She hoped he knew her better than that.

"It'll be fun," Carl assured her. He leaned closer as if to steal a kiss, and Camila found herself leaning closer to him, too.

"Ahem."

Camila jumped as if she'd been smacked—which her mother looked like she wanted to do. Carl looked from her to Paula and back again, and understanding dawned on his face. He sat back.

"Sorry. Your daughter just looked so sweet—"

"You will behave like a gentleman if you plan to escort Camila to her aunt and uncle's house," Paula decreed frostily.

"Yes, ma'am," Carl said. He looked at Camila and winked.

THEY LEFT WELL before noon, long before Diego and Mateo were due home from the restaurant, and Camila's mother promised to make up a cover story so her father didn't know where they were—or what they were doing.

"The gift of the mask must be a surprise," she said.

Camila's expression told Carl she wasn't sure if that was a good idea.

He figured he'd get the rest of the story when she was ready. Meantime, he meant to enjoy himself. At the airport, when they'd made it through security and found a fast-food place to purchase a quick meal, they sat together waiting for their plane to be called. He sent off a quick text to Sven, telling him about his sudden trip and assuring him he'd still call that night.

"Your mother likes me," he teased Camila. He'd

seen Paula taking in his expensive watch and leather luggage, and she'd let him accompany her daughter, even if his attempt to kiss Camila had offended her. Carl didn't hold her interest against her—or her strictness. Every parent should worry about their children's future. He had done his best to assure Paula he was in a strong postion to give Camila a secure life.

Camila waved that off, but a blush stained her cheeks. "Mom hasn't had things easy—"

"I know," Carl cut her off. "I really enjoyed meeting her."

"The way she asked you all those questions…"

"I didn't mind that," Carl assured her. "I like people who speak their minds. Makes me feel at home." His own parents had been hardworking, plainspoken people. He still missed them—a lot. His father had died of an aneurysm at fifty. His mother had passed away from cancer only three years later. Meanwhile, Carl had been building his business. He'd barely had time to process his loss. When he'd finally slowed down and thought about what he wanted in life, he'd realized a home base was the main thing. The kind of home his father had always longed for.

Speaking of which.

"Are you getting excited to go home? You were a teenager the last time you did this, right?" he asked Camila. If memory served, she'd moved to Houston when she was sixteen.

Camila didn't answer right away, and Carl glanced down to find her biting her lip. "Yeah," she said finally.

"Seems like a long time ago."

He wondered what was wrong. Did she miss Mexico more than he realized? Maybe she wished she was going back for good.

"So, what's the deal with this mask?" he asked to distract himself from the unsettling idea.

"It's an old Olmec heirloom—or that's the story, anyway. I don't know if it has any real monetary worth."

"Sometimes sentimental value is the most important kind there is." When he touched her arm, he realized how tense she was. He wondered why, but their flight was announced, and he didn't have time to press her.

They landed around midafternoon, collected their things at the airport in Toluca and boarded a bus.

"It's like another world," he said when they'd been riding some time, leaning to look out the window. He'd never been to Mexico, and if he was honest, he'd expected it to be an extension of Texas in terms of its terrain. In a way it was: a dry, desert environment full of cacti and brush. But it was different, too. In Texas there were vast unbroken spaces, but they always ended in a modern town or city with familiar high-rises and fast-food franchises. Here, all they passed through were towns that seemed straight out of the seventeenth century. That made the parts in between seem even vaster and emptier.

Camila seemed lost in thought as they moved through the landscape. Carl knew it must be strange coming home after all these years. He decided to leave her in peace, settled into his seat and pulled out his phone. He plugged in the headphones so she wouldn't hear what he was doing, then pulled up a language-learning app. Luckily he was a quick learner with an ear for languages, and he'd always been able to pick up a few phrases when doing business with foreigners. He hoped knowing at least a little Spanish would help out when he talked to her relatives.

When they finally pulled into Taxco, nearly three hours later, it looked nothing like Chance Creek. For one thing, this town was built into the side of a cliff, and tight, narrow, cobbled roads twisted up and down the side of the mountain. Built primarily of stone, the houses and shops reminded him of Rome more than anything he'd seen in the Americas. The colors jumped out at Carl. He wouldn't call Chance Creek a dull-looking town by any stretch, but its color palette was fairly tame: green grass, wood-paneled houses, blue jeans and flannel. The gray stone facades of Taxco's storefronts were painted a dizzying array of bright yellows, reds, oranges and greens, surrounded by trees that blossomed purple, red and blue. Stalls lined some of the wider streets and alleys, teeming with flowers and tropical fruits he couldn't begin to identify. The stall's proprietors, dressed in eclectic outfits that mixed modern styles with traditional ones, called out over the honks of passing cars and the cheerful birdsong ringing out from the eaves of a nearby church. As he and Camila disembarked, a crowd met the other passengers with shouted greetings, and Carl got the feeling every-one knew each other. Taxco and Chance Creek weren't that different, after all.

"Juana won't be here for nearly an hour," Camila said, consulting her phone. "Let's find something to eat for dinner first."

Carl picked up their bags and led the way down what appeared to be the main street. They passed through a street market, but none of the booths gave a clear indication of what they were selling, and Carl didn't see any food he recognized. At one point, Camila approached a stall and looked like she might place an order before she wrinkled her face and turned away. Carl pressed on. When they came to a restaurant that looked modern, and clean enough, he sighed in relief. The sign bore the word *barbacoa*, which he figured had to be Spanish for barbecue. Barbecue should be roughly the same anywhere, he figured.

"Let's try this place."

"Sure," Camila said uncertainly.

Inside, he couldn't see a host, and nobody approached them, so after standing there for an awkward minute, he grabbed the arm of a passing waiter. "A table—" He got a baffled look. Whoops. "Uh, *un mesa de doble, disculpe.*" The waiter blinked at him. Maybe he hadn't said that quite right.

"Una mesa para dos, por favor." Camila came to his rescue. He'd never heard her speak Spanish before, and he liked the way the lilting language tripped off her tongue. Something stirred deep within him, and he pictured the two of them in a far more intimate situation. Would Camila speak in Spanish to him then? It might be pretty

sexy.

He squashed the wayward thought. There was a time and a place—

And this wasn't it.

The waiter said something back to them and went on his way. Carl glanced at Camila, who translated. "We can sit anywhere."

Despite its small size, the restaurant was packed. Before they'd pulled out their chairs, a waiter materialized beside them. *"Bebidas?"*

There was something Carl could handle. Drinks. That language app was coming in handy. So was his exceptional memory. *"Agua, por favor."*

The waiter nodded. *"Jamaica? Tamarindo? Limonada?"*

Carl looked at Camila, out of his depth again.

"He's asking what kind of water you want."

"Uh… normal water?"

She grinned and repeated his request to the man. Just for a moment, Carl felt at ease. He'd always had fun with Camila. Even if he didn't speak the language, they could have a good time. But when the waiter handed them their menus, Carl sighed. He knew German, and a bit of Japanese, but he'd thought he'd recognize more of the food items after living in California so long. He knew tacos, of course, but what were *tacos dorados* or *tacos de cecina*? When he saw *tacos de barbacoa*, he gave up— he'd never heard of barbecued tacos.

The waiter came back with their drinks. Carl's water came in a bottle, which he accepted gratefully, aware that for a gringo, bottled water was safer. He decided to play it safe with his food order, too. *"Un hamburguesa,"* he said when the waiter came back. The waiter cocked his head. Carl tried again. *"Una. Una hamburguesa."*

Camila's giggle made him look up, and he chuckled, too, aware he was butchering the pronunciation.

"Una hamburguesa," she repeated to the waiter, pronouncing it "am-ber-gay-sa." Then she ordered something for herself that even he could understand: *fajitas de pollo con una ensalada.* Chicken fajitas with a side salad. Maybe he should have ordered that, too. When the waiter left, Camila smiled again.

"I didn't know you spoke Spanish," she said.

"I don't think that waiter knows it, either." Carl answered her grin with one of his own, and for a moment he felt like they were co-conspirators. Maybe this trip was exactly what they needed. Nothing like travel to bring two people together—

Or rip two people apart if they didn't belong together.

That was a sobering thought, and Carl decided he'd rise to any occasion this journey threw at them. He reached across the table to take Camila's hand. "Camila, I want you to know—"

His phone buzzed in his pocket, and Carl pulled it out by force of habit. Sven. He took the call with a sigh, letting go of Camila's hand and lifting a finger to let her know he'd be quick. "What's up?"

His friend sounded shaky. "I need you here, man."

Carl tamped down the flush of guilt that washed through him. He knew he should be in California with

Sven during the negotiations. "I'm… a little busy right now. I told you I'd call you later."

"This can't wait. I haven't heard from Fulsom. My employees are freaking out. Hell, I'm freaking out. How much do I tell them?"

"Don't tell them anything. Fulsom's trying to rattle you, and it's working. Next thing you know you'll be calling him. That's what he wants—you begging him to buy your company. You have to realize this is all a game to him, and you need to keep your head on straight and play it like a game, too. Do nothing. Make no attempt to communicate with Fulsom. Go about your business as usual. Tell your people you'll pass on the information they need when you have it."

"But—"

"Sven, here's the deal. Fulsom won't send you an offer until right before his deadline. He knows by then you'll be shaking in your boots. I'll most likely be there by the time you get it—and if not, call me and I'll talk you through it from here."

"Promise?"

"Promise." He hoped he was right.

"What was that all about?" Camila asked when he hung up.

"A friend. Sven Andersson. I mentored him for a number of years. His company took off, and now it's being bought out for an astronomical sum. Another Silicon Valley millionaire in the making."

"That's great."

"It is great. The only thing is, I'll need to fly out

there for a couple of days when we're done here. But after the deal's done, my business in California is over. For good." He took her hand again and held it. "I mean that, Camila."

"Really?" She brightened.

"Really." He'd be firm with Sven on that point. No more being pulled between two worlds.

When their food arrived, Carl decided hamburgers were the perfect thing to order in Mexico, after all. This one was just the way a hamburger should be—tender and succulent. He wasn't sure about Camila's dinner, though. There was chicken on her plate, but the fajita part seemed to be missing—until the waiter brought by tortillas and several salsas. Her salad was made of some vegetable he didn't recognize, something dark green and fleshy, almost like artichoke hearts. Like the chicken, it was cut into long, thin strips.

Carl took another bite of his burger, then cursed and dropped it as a searing heat burned his tongue. He grabbed his water and gulped down half the contents in its plastic bottle.

"Hay un problema, señor?" A waiter rushed to Carl's side.

"Carl? Are you okay?" Camila asked.

Coughing and sputtering, he lifted the bun of his hamburger to show her. "There's a hot pepper on my burger! A jalapeño or something!"

Camila translated, and the waiter broke into a grin. "No no no, no, señor, no hay. Este es cuaresmeño, más sabor, muy rico."

Camila frowned. "He says it's not jalapeño. It's a *cuaresmeño.*"

Carl plucked the offending slices of pepper off his burger, but his mouth still burned too badly to enjoy the rest of the meal. Camila kept biting back smiles, which didn't help. He hated being the gringo who couldn't handle spicy food. Great impression he was making.

When five men filed in carrying instruments and began to play not three feet from where they sat, he had had enough.

At least the bill was a pleasant surprise. Carl did the math in his head. Barely four American dollars for a full meal for two. He could certainly afford that, he thought with a private chuckle.

They were late to the place they were to meet Juana, and when they finally did arrive, Camila's cousin wasn't there. Carl checked his phone, worried they had missed her. It was almost twenty minutes past the agreed-upon time.

"Maybe this is the wrong place," Camila said.

Carl shook his head. "I'm pretty sure this is it."

"Maybe she isn't coming." She sounded discouraged.

Carl put an arm around her shoulders and was pleased when she leaned into him. "She'll come." He didn't mind if Camila's cousin was late if he got to be close to Camila, but if she'd already been and gone—that might be a problem.

"I'm sorry," she said. "This is just all a lot to take—"

"You're coming home again after so many years. I

understand. Seeing your family again—"

She pulled back suddenly, and Carl reluctantly let her go.

"Yeah. It's... weird." She dried her eyes and turned away, scanning the street for any sign of her cousin.

Carl studied her, wondering why she'd pulled away. It had felt good to hold her in his arms, but something always interrupted them just when they got close, and that frustrated him.

When Juana arrived a full twenty minutes later, he breathed a sigh of relief that they wouldn't have to try to rent a car and navigate to Camila's family's ranch in the coming darkness. Juana hopped out of the car. *"Buenos tardes, buenos tardes, mi prima."*

Camila tried to shake her hand and got tangled up when her cousin went in for a stiff, formal kiss on the cheek. When the young woman turned to Carl, he was prepared. He moved in for a similar kiss but stumbled when Juana stepped quickly out of his reach. She was tall and slim, as pretty as a model and as haughty, too.

"Quíen es?" she demanded of Camila.

"This is Carl Whitfield," Camila told her. "My... friend. Mom told your mother he was coming. Carl, this is my cousin, Juana."

Juana frowned. "Juana Sofía Valentín Torres." She emphasized the last three names as if put out Camila had forgotten to mention them.

Carl wasn't sure what that was all about, and he didn't have time to ask questions, either. Juana quickly hustled them into her car and began to drive, speaking quickly in Spanish until Camila said something, and Juana switched to a heavily accented English. As they drove over the dry terrain, the sun fading in the west, Carl focused on the women's conversation, itching to take the wheel himself and let them talk. He wasn't used to being a passenger.

"How is Aunt Ximena? I'm looking forward to seeing her," Camila said rather formally. Carl was surprised how stiff the cousins seemed with each other. Juana looked to be a similar age to Camila, and he assumed they'd grown up together, but she sat ramrod straight in her seat and kept her eyes on the road. Maybe all the years Camila lived in the States had created an awkwardness between them.

"She's fine. She sends her greetings. She'll see you when she gets home."

Camila shared a startled glance with Carl. "Gets home? Where is she?" Why hadn't her mother told her Ximena was away?

"At Cousin Delfina's, in Day Effay." Noticing their confusion, she added, "Ciudad de México."

Camila nodded and looked back at Carl in the back seat. "It's in Mexico City."

Juana laughed, a musical sound. "Don't mess with the gringo, Camila. Day Effay. DF. It's not *in* Mexico City; it *is* Mexico City," she told Carl.

Was it his imagination, or was Camila blushing? Had she been messing with him? She must have known what Juana meant all along.

He shrugged it off. "Go right ahead and tease the

gringo," he told Camila with a smile.

"I wasn't trying to—"

Juana cut her off. "DF stands for Distrito Federal, which is the federal district where Mexico City is. But the city takes up the whole district, and it is the only federal district there is, so we just call the city that now."

Carl caught the gleam in Juana's eye when she met his eye in the rearview mirror. She enjoyed having the upper hand. He nodded at her explanation but kept his mouth shut the rest of the way, unsure about the undercurrents running between the two women and unwilling to provoke Juana further. She seemed the prickly sort. The conversation died down without his input, and they rode in silence. Just like on the bus, Camila seemed drawn by the landscape, searching it with her gaze as if looking for an answer to a mystery.

Carl tried to squelch the uneasiness rising inside him again. Camila had settled in Montana. She had friends and a business there. She wouldn't want to give that all up, even if Mexico was obviously calling to her.

At least, he hoped not.

It was dark when they reached the ranch. Carl climbed out of the car and breathed in a familiar earthy smell that had almost put him off owning a ranch at all when he'd first come to Montana. He'd never have believed back then dirt and manure and animal sweat could smell so sweet to him now.

Like the houses in Taxco, Juana's home was made mostly of stone, with cracked and dusty walls that looked as old as history itself. They passed first through a picket fence that enclosed the fields surrounding the ranch, then an outer stone wall that enclosed a series of wide courtyards. The main building was built into the structure of the outer wall, whereas the outbuildings were scattered about the courtyards—Carl supposed that made them inbuildings.

They met Juana's brother in the kitchen. Juana introduced him as Luis Pedro Valentín Torres, and Carl dearly hoped he wasn't expected to remember four names for every relative. Luis crossed the room quickly to give Camila a big hug and a kiss on the cheek. *"Bienvenido,"* he said, *"buenas tardes."* While they embraced, Carl glanced at a shelf across the room, above a large table, where a deep green, solid stone face stared down at them. Was that the mask they'd come here to get?

It had narrowed eyes and downturned lips, and Carl got the impression it disapproved of him, but that was just the way it was carved. Everyone probably felt the same thing when they looked at it.

Still, he was relieved when Luis came to greet him. Carl returned the greeting warmly but got a long, appraising look in return. *"Él está con Señor Valenzuela?"* the man asked Camila suddenly.

"He's with me, Luis," Camila said. She looked at Juana. "Who is Valenzuela?"

It was Luis who answered. "Señor Valenzuela is a man of business in Acapulco. He owns all this—" he spread his arms wide to encompass the whole property "—and so he owns all of us, but he does not care for us, for our *hacienda*. He is rich, powerful. What is one small ranch to him?" He looked Carl up and down, taking in his pressed shirt and his expensive watch. "I think that you would be friends."

CAMILA HAD BEEN overwhelmed on the bus as she watched the desert plains of Estado de México give way to the forested valleys of Morelos and finally the grand rolling hills of Guerrero as the sun slipped below the horizon. Now her aunt and uncle's house was stirring something inside her she couldn't name. It was like a primitive memory, even though she'd never been here before. She wanted to look at everything, but she didn't want to be impolite.

When they'd gotten off the bus in Taxco, and there'd been no one there to greet them, it seemed achingly obvious she didn't belong. She knew no one, and no one knew her. She'd wanted to stop at the street vendors but had been afraid she'd make some ridiculous mistake. When she'd heard a vendor shouting words she'd recognized—whatever he was pedaling was roasted in lime, dressed with salt and honey—she'd gone closer and found boxes full of what looked like roasted nuts. The sign read *"Chapulines"*—not a Spanish word but Nahuatl, unless she was mistaken. They smelled amazing. She was about to call out to Carl when she realized a million caramelized eyes were staring back at her.

Crickets. Whole roasted crickets.

After that she'd let Carl call the shots.

She still felt off-balance as she greeted the members of her extended family, familiar from dozens of photographs, emails, phone calls and her parents' stories. She cast a glance at Carl. As he shook hands with her uncle Gerardo, who'd stayed behind while her aunt was visiting family, the enormity of the task she'd undertaken overwhelmed her. How was she supposed to wrest something from her own family they didn't want to give up? It hadn't been fair of her mother to give her this job. Definitely hadn't been fair of her to send her when Ximena wasn't even at home.

But there was no going back now.

Shaking off her dark thoughts, Camila moved to greet her uncle, too, but Juana stepped in her way. "Why don't you tell us why you are really here?"

"Juana," Uncle Gerardo said, but Camila figured she might as well tell them. She switched to Spanish. Carl didn't need to hear the family's dirty laundry.

"*Mamá* sent me," she told them. "She wants the mask to give to *Papá* for his birthday. He's missing his home and she wants to cheer him up." She glanced up to where the green jade object sat on its shelf. It stared disdainfully back.

Juana snorted and answered in Spanish, as well. "If you're here for the mask, this is all a waste of time. Might as well run on home."

"Juanita." Luis gave her a brotherly shove. "Stay as long as you like," he told Camila. "We're happy to have you." When he spoke to Carl, he switched to English, his tone perfectly polite but flat. "You also may stay. We are pleased to welcome you."

At least Camila had one friend here. She gave Luis a sincere smile. "Thank you."

"But Juana's right," he said, switching back to Spanish. "We can't give you the mask to take to Houston. It belongs to Mexico. It will stay in Mexico." His pronouncement was as final as Juana's.

"He's right," Gerardo added. "Ximena insists on it."

"Not just *Mamá*." Juana nodded. She narrowed her eyes at Camila. "The mask knows its place. I don't suppose you've studied its history? Our history?"

Camila had, but she had a feeling her knowledge wouldn't stand up to Juana's grilling.

"I thought not. Countless owners of the mask have fought and died for Mexico. Cuauhtemoc himself—"

Camila couldn't help but laugh. "Cuauhtemoc himself?" she parroted. That part of the story had to be a myth—he was an ancient Aztec warrior.

Juana frowned. "Cuauhtemoc himself once carried the mask with him into battle. And now you want to take it from the country our ancestors gave their lives for?" She looked Camila up and down. "Gringa. Your family left. You clearly aren't interested in our country. Why steal something that doesn't matter one cucumber to you?"

"That's not fair. I didn't choose where I was born—" Was Juana seriously berating her for decisions her parents had made? But as much as Juana's accusations hurt, Camila couldn't pretend she'd expected anything less. Of course Juana looked down on her. How could she ever live up to the standards of the perfect Mexican daughter?

"Did she say Cuauhtemoc? The Aztec emperor?" Carl asked, and Camila blessed him for the interruption but was anxious about what he'd say next. What could he possibly contribute to this conversation that wouldn't make things worse?

To Camila's surprise, Luis laughed. "We were speaking of our history," he said in English. "Some give the accounts more credit than others. Hard to know what to believe."

"Carl isn't interested in our history," Camila said. "And it's been a long day." She'd had enough of this.

"Of course it has. Juana, show our guests their rooms," Gerardo said.

Juana huffed but obeyed her father and led the way.

Carl took Camila's hand and followed her.

Camila curled her fingers around his gratefully. She'd been right to let Carl come along, an ally among these adversaries. She'd managed to avoid a blowout with her cousins tonight, but she had a feeling things were going to get ugly before this trip was done.

Chapter Four

THAT HADN'T GONE so badly, Carl thought as he followed Camila and Juana down a narrow hall. He liked Luis and Gerardo, and while he hadn't been able to keep up with the conversation, he figured he'd done his best. He was glad he'd brought some casual clothes he could work in. First thing tomorrow he meant to pitch in and help around the ranch. Luckily he'd had a lot of practice at that these past few years.

Outside the windows of the house, it was fully dark, and Carl was surprised how late it had gotten, but when he checked his watch he realized it wasn't even eight. They were far closer to the equator here than they were up in Montana, he remembered.

Juana stopped at the entrance to a small room. "Camila." She waved a hand for Camila to enter the room but blocked the way when Carl went to follow. "For Camila," she reiterated.

Of course. He hadn't meant to assume they'd share it, but before he could say this, Juana crossed her arms and faced her cousin. "*Que indecente*. Such an assumption for him to make. Are you sleeping with him outside marriage? No true Torres would act like that."

Camila winced, and Carl blinked. "Watch it—" he started.

"*Mamá* will be home tomorrow. She would die to see such indecency," Juana went on.

He'd heard enough. "First of all—"

"Carl, it's okay." Camila slipped in between them. "Juana, neither of us meant any disrespect. And Carl and I aren't sleeping together, not that it's any of your business."

"You're a member of my family; that makes it my business. Come. I'll show you your room," Juana said to Carl. "Be glad I still give you one after you disrespect my cousin so." She led the way back down the hall. Carl glanced back at Camila, who seemed caught between laughter and exasperation.

"See you in the morning," she said with a shake of her head. Carl followed Juana, trying to cling to the remains of his sanity.

It wouldn't do to show weakness to the enemy.

His phone buzzed in his pocket just as Juana escorted him into a small, neat bedroom at the back of the house. She left without another word, her displeasure clear in every gesture. Carl sighed, shut the door and answered the call.

"How much progress have you made so far?" Virginia Cooper demanded.

Carl kneaded the back of his neck with one hand. He shouldn't have answered the phone. "No more since the last time we talked. I'm in Mexico."

"Mexico?" The mixture of outrage and disbelief in

her voice implied she'd never heard of such a thing. "The way you flit around, no wonder you can't find a home in Chance Creek."

Ouch. "I'll be back in a couple of days. I'll work on the presentation here, then finish it when I get back. I'm heading to California on the eighth to meet with Sven, the man who'll help with the funding and the robotics program."

"California, huh? I see where your priorities are."

"My priorities are keeping the promises I've made."

"You'd better keep the one you made to me. Get that presentation done. We need time to look it over well before the twelfth. I thought you were a businessman."

"I am." Or he was. Now he was a rancher. A rancher without a ranch… "And I understand you're anxious to get started," he said, knowing he needed to placate Virginia. "I have to hammer a few things out with Sven before I can get too far."

Virginia sniffed. "The architect has already finished his part. If you weren't dragging your feet on your end, construction could be underway by now. You don't seem all that interested in getting a ranch."

"I'm interested," he assured her. There was no way construction could have started under any circumstances, but he wasn't going to argue it out tonight. "I'll get on it, Virginia, as soon as I can." He hung up. Time to call Sven.

It was relatively early in California, and his friend was still at his office. Without being interrupted, they were able to go over different deals Fulsom might offer and the responses Sven could give to them, and Sven calmed down, which was a good thing. He needed to be sharp during negotiations. By the time Carl had said goodbye, they'd gotten a basic strategy in place and mapped out an action plan for once the offer had been made.

"Stay strong," Carl told Sven. "Don't blink. When the offer comes, don't rush to answer it. We have time to think things through."

"Will do. Thanks, Carl. I mean it; I know you've got your own life going on."

"I'm doing my best to take care of both. Talk to you tomorrow. When we do we'd better start hammering out this presentation I need to write for Virginia."

"I'll make some notes while I'm pacing my office tonight," Sven joked.

When they'd hung up, Carl stripped down, climbed into bed and started on the language app again. He'd been proud of how many phrases he'd learned during their short flight, but it was all too clear he had a long way to go.

He only completed a few more lessons before his head began to swim, however, and he used his data to bring up a search engine. He'd heard of Cuauhtémoc, and of the Aztecs, but much of the earlier conversation between Juana and Camila had eluded him. Before the Europeans, Mexico was divided between the Mayan and Aztec empires, right? Or was it the Aztecs and the Incas? In any case, he'd never heard of the Olmecs or the Nahuatl.

He settled into the challenge of finding answers. He was good at memorizing information, but he was better at solving puzzles. It wasn't fancy shirts or expensive watches that had defined him in his earlier life; it was tackling new challenges head on with tireless enthusiasm.

He missed that.

Carl considered the past few years. He'd enjoyed learning about ranching from the Coopers, and the physical work felt great after years at a desk job, but he missed coming up with a vision and carrying it through. He wouldn't get to experience that part of ranching until he owned his own spread, which made him even more eager to make that happen.

He'd done all he could on that front right now, though. A quick look at listings earlier had told him nothing new had come on the market.

He settled down to the task at hand.

Three thousand years before the dawn of the Nahuatl, or Aztec, Empire, the precursors of the Teotihuacán people settled in Cuicuilco, the article began, and Carl realized as he took in the unfamiliar sounds of the Torres ranch he probably wasn't going to sleep much in his new surroundings tonight. That was a given anyway, though.

If he hadn't been thinking about precolonial Mesoamerica, he'd be thinking of Camila—and exactly what they'd do together when they finally got alone.

NOW SHE KNEW what her cousin thought of her.

Camila worked in silence, unpacking her suitcase and settling into her new room. Juana had come back to help her, and Camila pointedly ignored her in the hopes that she'd get the hint and go away.

Juana's assertion she wasn't a true Torres—and therefore not a true Mexican—struck home. It cut far too close for comfort to her father's lectures when she was a child growing up.

Diego had always emphasized the distinction between true Mexicans and the Americanized versions. He had wanted to raise children who stayed close to their roots, so they'd spoken Spanish daily, eaten traditional food, and her father had regaled them with stories about their history—when he had time. Unfortunately, running the restaurant left little of that, leaving the information in Camila's head full of holes.

It wasn't her fault she wasn't born and raised here, and Juana's accusation wouldn't hurt so much if her father hadn't made such a fuss about authenticity, too. He hated the way her friends in Houston spoke a mixture of Spanish and English, the meanings of traditional words changed by such close contact with another language. He hated the music she'd listened to, which combined Spanish lyrics with American rock and roll.

He despised the Americanized Mexican food served in restaurants—

Just the mention of a hard-shell taco could send her father into a furious tirade.

For Juana to call out Camila on her heritage was a

direct insult.

Camila couldn't think of a suitable answer.

Meanwhile, Juana stared at each item Camila unpacked as if its presence in the room might taint her. As Camila put away the last of her clothes, Juana frowned at something in the bottom of the suitcase. "What is this?" She fished it out between two fingers, as if it might bite.

Camila recognized the photograph she'd brought to Houston to show her parents—an image she'd taken the day she and Fila opened their restaurant.

"Fila's Familia," Juana read out loud, echoing the sign that hung over the restaurant's entry. "Afghan-Mexican fusion food." She laughed derisively. "Afghan-Mexican food? What is that? You poor thing, if this is all there is to eat in Montana. Just wait until I have the chance to cook for you. You'll want to never go back."

Camila snatched the photo back. "That's my restaurant. And Afghan-Mexican food is delicious!"

Juana's mouth twisted as if she'd swallowed something sour. "*Your* restaurant," she repeated. "Huh."

Camila reached her breaking point. "You know what? I've had a long day, and I'd like to be alone." She crossed the room and opened the door pointedly. After a moment Juana followed her.

"Of course," Juana hissed. "The gringa doesn't want a real Mexican around." She flung herself out of the room.

Camila shut the door behind her and sat down on the bed. Couldn't anyone in her family be proud of her accomplishments? It was as if she could never be good enough. Certainly not as good as perfect Juana, who thought Camila was some kind of a traitor to Mexico.

They'd treated her like a thief for even asking for the mask—as if she was the one after it and not her mother.

Camila picked up the photograph and put it away in her bag. She couldn't wait to get home to Chance Creek.

As if on cue, her phone buzzed.

Maya again.

Those Coopers are definitely up to something. Virginia Cooper's so smug these days you'd think she was about to be crowned queen! Liam's riled as a wet hen. He's stuck on the ranch unless one of us drives him. It's like having a delinquent child.

What do you think Virginia's up to? Camila typed back. Hearing Chance Creek gossip made her even more homesick.

I don't know—I hoped you would. I heard Carl's out of town again. Where do you think he went?

How should I know? Camila wrote back quickly. She didn't want Maya thinking she was helping the Coopers.

You guys hear everything at the restaurant.

I'm not at the restaurant. Gotta go, Camila texted back and turned off her phone.

CARL WOKE WELL before dawn, rose from his bed, pulled on jeans and a T-shirt, slipped his feet into his boots, grabbed his hat and headed to the kitchen, where Luis and a couple of the other men were already up and about. Old habits died hard, and even though he hadn't gotten much sleep last night, he knew once he was awake he'd stay that way. Besides, he wanted to help Camila.

"Oye," one of them shouted from the table. "Gringo *rico*, where has your *ropa de marca* gone?"

Before Carl could think of a response to a question he didn't understand, Luis pressed a steaming mug of coffee into one hand and a plate of what looked like fried corn husks into the other. "That's my brother, Arturo David Valentín Torres." Luis indicated the seated man and pointed to a chair. Carl sat down, too. Arturo was taller than Luis, huskier, too, but the men shared the same dark hair and quick smiles.

"I'm Carl." He shook Arturo's hand. "Nice to meet you."

"Salsa?" Arturo slid some jars his way, none of which looked like what Carl thought of as salsa. "Salt. Cilantro. Where are your fancy clothes, Carlos?"

"Atole?" Luis offered him a pitcher of something milky, white and steaming.

"Uh, no thanks." He turned back to Arturo. "It's Carl, not Carlos. And I didn't think I would need my fancy clothes today."

"My mistake," said Arturo, though his grin said it hadn't been. "You remind me of Señor Slim."

"Carlos Slim?" Carl chuckled. The comparison was flattering. The world's richest man had informed some of his own entrepreneurial strategies.

"A smart man," Luis said. "Sugar for your coffee?

Cream?"

Arturo snorted. "A smart devil."

"One cream is fine. Slim's not popular here?" Carl had always assumed he would be about equivalent to a Bill Gates or Warren Buffett figure in Mexico.

"Depends who you ask," Luis said, pouring Carl's cream for him.

"And how much of his money is in their pocket," Arturo growled. "Eat your tamales, gringo."

Carl took a bite. The cornmeal was rather bland. Luckily the coffee was strong and dark.

"I'd like to help out today."

"The gringo knows ranching?" Arturo scoffed.

"The gringo does," Carl told him.

"We'll be moving the cattle right after we eat," Luis said. "Borrow a horse and join us."

"Will do." After draining his mug, Carl finished his meal quickly, grateful when Camila came into the kitchen. He had the feeling she'd been up earlier than he had. There were dark smudges under her eyes, and she was moving slowly. When her gaze lit on the coffeepot, she perked up.

He wondered if she'd slept at all.

He brought his dishes to the sink and asked her in a low voice, "What's the plan?"

"I don't know," she admitted. "My cousins aren't going to give me the mask. Maybe when my aunt gets here, I'll have better luck with her. I have to wait for her to get back."

How long would that be? Carl tried to hide his consternation, but he must have failed.

"You don't have to stay," Camila told him. "I know you're busy." She turned away.

Hell, Carl thought. "I want to stay," he said truthfully, pursuing her. He was finally getting a chance to spend some time with her. If it hadn't been for losing the Hilltop Acres, this mission would easily be his top priority.

Her relief was palpable. "I appreciate it." She touched his hand, and Carl's body woke up. He was always aware of Camila on a physical level, but when she got close, he felt more alive than at any other time.

Someday he'd get Camila alone, and he'd get as close to her as two humans could get.

But he'd better stop thinking about that now before he gave himself away.

"I'm not going anywhere," he promised and hoped he could live up to his words. "In the meantime, how about I help the menfolk outside, and you work on Juana? Maybe if we butter them up, they'll change their minds."

Camila snorted. "It's worth a try, but don't hold your breath."

Carl stepped outside a few minutes later, and his optimism returned. Dawn was coming, but the sun hadn't broken over the horizon yet. The day seemed fresh and new and full of possibilities. Camila's mother wouldn't have sent her if she didn't think Camila could complete her errand. It made sense that Ximena, Diego's sister, would be the one to decide whether the mask stayed or went. In the meantime, his first measure of business was to make himself useful. It was a beautiful morning, and if the ranch was laid out somewhat differently than they usually were in Montana, that was fine. He admired the enclosures filled with hundreds of chickens, the pens of goats and the fields of corn, rows of tomatoes and orchards of apple, mango and avocado trees.

Carl didn't know how to take care of avocado trees or goats, but he sure as hell knew his way around a herd of cattle. He found a horse in the nearby stables, saddled up and rode out to the cattle enclosure. There were several larger pastures nearby, and given the arid landscape and the hundreds of hoofprints leading toward them, he figured the Torres family rotated the cattle through them. One looked very dry, but if he drove them through the other gate, the cattle could reach the creek far down at the bottom of the hill. Given the clear sky overhead, he figured that was the better option. It was already getting hot. He threw open the gate and started urging the cattle toward the hillside.

He'd gotten the herd well on their way when the rest of the men came out to watch him. Arturo shouted after him, "Where are you taking our cattle, gringo *rico*?"

Carl pulled his horse up and shouted back, "They need water, don't they?"

Arturo threw his hands up in the air. "Gringo loco!"

Luis pursued Carl. "No need to take them to the creek. Rain today, and lots of it. We'll keep them close."

"Are you sure?"

"I'm sure," Luis confirmed.

Carl didn't think he could be right, but he wanted to make a good impression on these men, so he decided the last thing he should do was tell them how to run their ranch. Instead, he helped them herd the cattle back into the closer enclosure, and though they teased him about his mistake, he got the feeling it was all in fun. Even Arturo seemed friendlier now that Carl had messed up.

They spent the next two hours mending fences, another task Carl was quite familiar with, until fierce black clouds covered the sky. The temperature plummeted, and Carl ran for the safety of the barn with the others when rain fell hard all around them. Lightning split the sky, and thunder roared so close the rafters shook with it.

He could only imagine how fast the creek would rise after such a storm. If he'd gotten those cows down the slope, it might have been a disaster.

So much for knowing how to ranch.

He hoped no one told Camila about his mistake.

"I'LL BE BACK to make breakfast," Juana said when the dishes were done. "You go… rest."

"We just ate breakfast."

Juana rolled her eyes. "That was a snack for the menfolk to keep them going through their first chores. Real breakfast comes later." She disappeared to her room, leaving Camila in the kitchen alone.

But Camila had no intention of resting. Here was

her chance to prove herself. She wouldn't be a guest; she'd be a helper. When Juana came back, she'd have a satisfying meal all prepared. But what should she make?

She wished she could prepare something fancy, but that wasn't practical. She didn't know what ingredients and equipment the kitchen stocked, didn't know how heat diffused across this particular stovetop or how the altitude and dry air would affect the cooking process. Chances were she'd just embarrass herself. Better to start simple: she'd make *huevos rancheros*, something even a child could get right.

Camila got the eggs ready and sliced the avocados before she encountered her first hiccup. It was time to make the tortillas, but she couldn't find any masa flour. There were a couple of unmarked jars whose contents looked close, but the grains were far coarser than what she was used to. She decided she would hold off on the tortillas until everything else was finished and started on the salsa instead.

She'd just finished dicing the tomatoes when Juana appeared.

"What are you doing?"

Camila kept her cool. "Making huevos rancheros."

Juana raised her eyebrows. "Huevos rancheros? What are the avocados for? And the sugar?"

Camila rolled her eyes. "The sugar is for the salsa."

"Salsa de que?"

"What?"

"What kind of salsa?" Juana peered into the bowl where Camila was mixing the tomatoes with oil, sugar, cilantro, salt, pepper and peppers. "Italian pasta salsa, by the looks of it."

Camila crossed her arms. Juana was being deliberately obtuse. *Salsa* might simply mean sauce here in Mexico, but she had to know it meant something far more precise in the United States. "Do you need something?" she asked pointedly. So much for feeling helpful.

"I need a nice breakfast, which means huevos rancheros that have not been made ruined with avocados and salsa gringa." Juana opened a cupboard, took out an old-fashioned mortar and pestle, and started making a sauce of her own. She left out the oil, sugar and pepper, went a little heavier on the chiles, then added a flurry of spices that Camila didn't catch and topped it off with freshly squeezed lime juice. "Try."

Camila took the spoonful Juana offered her. It was spicy—and really good.

But that didn't excuse her cousin's rudeness.

"The gringa doesn't even know how to cook," Juana said, elbowing Camila out of the way.

Camila lost what little patience she had left. "Then why am I the one who owns a restaurant? You've never even worked in one."

Juana jerked like she'd been slapped, and Camila wished she could take back her hasty words, but it was too late.

"Maybe not," Juana told her. "But I slave in this kitchen every day of my life, making *real* food my family can be proud of. *Mamá* says that *Tío* and *Tía* won't even try your fusion trash."

Camila's remorse evaporated, and she didn't know what she'd have said if the front door hadn't swung open just then.

Expecting the men back from the fields, she was surprised when an older woman entered the kitchen dressed in dark pants and a vibrant tunic, large silver jewelry gracing her throat and wrists. Her hair, beginning to silver but still very dark, was as stylish as her clothing.

"Mamá!" Juana cried.

Ximena was home.

Chapter Five

"**Y**OU OWN A ranch in Montana—where Camila is living now?" Arturo asked as they worked. Carl, breathing hard, struggled to answer. He was no stranger to hard work, but they were about 7,000 feet higher above sea level than he was used to. "I don't own it; I just work it, like you. I've been looking for one to buy. Hard to find a good one, though. This is a beautiful spread you've got here."

Arturo became somber. "You should give thanks, Carl, that at least you have the chance to buy a ranch, good or no. We will never own our home, and so we will never have the power to make it good."

Carl frowned. "If there are issues, can't you bring them up with the owner? I'm sure he wants the ranch to turn a profit more than anyone."

They were all silent for a long moment. Finally Luis spoke. "Perhaps, if we ever had the chance. Señor Valenzuela has never set foot on the property, although his intermediaries come often enough to enforce his rules and collect his payments. We have lodged our complaints with them but never get any response."

"That's not the way I'd do things if I owned a

ranch." Carl understood their disgust. "I intend to work my spread with my own two hands."

"That's because you're a rancher, not a businessman," Luis pronounced. He clapped Carl on the back, but Carl's answer caught in his throat. No matter what Luis thought, he was more businessman than rancher, even now. Called away to California every other week. Caught between two worlds. Helping Sven with the buyout really had to be the end of it. For Camila's sake—and his own. He couldn't run a ranch if he was going to leave it all the time.

"Come on," Luis said, breaking into his thoughts. "We have more to do before we head in for breakfast."

Carl welcomed the interruption. He'd sort out his future later.

"Coming," he said.

"AY, NIÑITA, AT long last!" Rather than the formal kiss Camila had received from Juana, Ximena treated her to a full body hug, squeezing her like a boa constrictor. When she was done, she reached for Juana again, lifting her daughter in the air and spinning her around.

"Mamá!" Juana disentangled herself, blushing and fixing her hair with all the affronted dignity of a teenager.

Ximena spotted the breakfast Camila had begun to prepare, looked it over, eyebrows raised, washed her hands, found an apron and got to work finishing it. She issued directions to both Camila and Juana, making a version of huevos rancheros somewhere between

Camila's original version and Juana's intended one. If she was as surprised as Juana was by the way Camila cooked, she didn't comment on it, and Camila appreciated that. She had gotten enough flack from her cousin.

When the men came in from outside, their clothes still damp from the sudden storm that had whipped up earlier, Camila was grateful for the interruption. With obvious reluctance, Juana introduced her mother to Carl as "Isabel Ximena Torres Arroyo."

The men took their seats at the table, and Ximena kept up a running commentary as she fussed over the food. "Eggs with avocado?" she asked when she got to the slices Camila had prepared. "How exciting. Come, *niñas*, or would you make an old lady set the table all alone? There, good. *Oye*, where are the tortillas? Don't tell me you meant to serve huevos rancheros without tortillas?" She threw up her hands in mock horror. "Maybe you've run out of corn where you come from, is that it? Is there a shortage? I hear you put corn in your cars in place of gas, trying to stop global warming, but at what cost? Better to let the world burn, I say, and let us bake our tortillas on the ashes."

Camila laughed and met Carl's gaze. He grinned back at her, obviously enjoying Ximena's banter as much as she was.

"I hear also, *cariña*," Ximena went on when they had all taken their seats, "that you are running a successful business now. Please, you must tell me all about this."

"Stop it." Juana slapped a flat hand on the table, speaking in Spanish, her words tumbling over themselves. "You don't know why she's here. It's not to visit us, *Mamá*. It's to steal our mask! She wants to take it back to Texas. Texas, *Mamá*, the very land the gringos stole from us. And this 'successful business' of hers? This Afghan-Mexican fusion restaurant, whatever that is? A mockery of our whole country."

"That's enough of that." Ximena turned stern in an instant, and she spoke deliberately in English so even Carl could understand. "Camila is a guest in our house, and she is our family. You will treat her with respect. Understand?"

"Yes, *Mamá*." Juana's expression was mutinous, but she nodded dutifully.

Ximena beamed. "We will speak about the mask later," she promised. "As for your most inventive cuisine, Camila, we all look forward to trying it." She winked. "Just because something is new does not mean it is not good."

The men went right back to work when breakfast was over, while Camila stayed to help Ximena and Juana with the cleanup, dreading the conversation with Ximena about the mask. At least her aunt hadn't erupted into anger as soon as she'd heard about it. In fact, she didn't seem all that surprised.

As soon as breakfast was cleaned up, Ximena and Juana jumped right into preparing lunch. Camila did what she could to help. If it had only been her and her aunt in the kitchen cooking, she would have had a blast watching Ximena cook. Unfortunately, Juana kept close the whole time, her rolling eyes and pinched lips telling

Camila exactly how little she thought of her gringa
cousin.

Ximena laughed, chatted and even sung snatches of
songs Camila half recognized as she worked. Camila
tried to ignore Juana. She wished Ximena would send
her daughter away, but Juana made sure to smile
whenever her mother's gaze fell upon her.

Ximena never mentioned the mask, and Camila
didn't know how to bring it up with Juana around. She
decided to wait until later and in the meantime welcomed the chance to get to know her aunt.

Still, it irked her to have Juana laugh at her igno-
rance every time she made a mistake, and it dawned on
Camila she'd had no idea how much she didn't know
about true Mexican cuisine. It wasn't her fault; despite
his tirades against the Americanization of their culture,
her father had obviously Americanized the food he
served at his *authentic* Mexican restaurant. Not to the
extent of serving hard-shell tacos, maybe, but he'd
tamed the heat level of his salsas, made use of American
cheeses rather than Mexican ones and made other
substitutions that would keep his customers happy.
How ironic she'd tried to prove her authenticity as a
chef to her father by cooking in the inauthentic way
he'd taught her.

The only thing that kept her sane was knowing soon
this would all be over. She'd persuade Ximena to hand
over the mask and fly back to Houston.

She didn't even want to think what would happen if
Ximena said no.

CARL MOPPED THE sweat from his brow, watching the sun—which had come out after the thunderstorm ended and burned bright and hot the rest of the day— set over the rolling hills of Guerrero. The hard day's work had restored his sense of confidence in his ranching skills. Not everything he'd learned from the Coopers translated to the way things were done here, but enough did that he'd been able to carry his own weight. All the while, new ideas were taking hold in his brain—ways to do things he hadn't come across in Montana.

He hadn't seen Camila since lunch. Carl smiled, re- membering Ximena's easy humor. Ximena seemed more like Camila than either Diego or Paula. A lightbulb went off in his brain. Camila had told him she didn't know why her mother had sent her here instead of one of her siblings. Now Carl thought he understood. Paula figured Camila was the one who could get Ximena to part with it.

His future mother-in-law was sneaky.

"Hungry?" Arturo asked, coming up beside him.

Carl nodded. "Starved."

"Good," said Luis, already turning toward the house. "Tonight, we dine on pozole, I hear." He went on ahead of them.

"The food's so good here, Camila must sometimes wish she'd never left home," Carl said.

Arturo gave him a funny look, and Carl figured something must have been lost in translation. He tried again. "She must want to come back and live here where she was born."

"Back? She's never been here before," Arturo told him. "She was born in Houston. Good thing you brought her here to visit, even if she is trying to take our mask."

"What's the deal with that, anyway?" Carl asked to cover his confusion. He was sure Camila had told him she was born in Mexico.

"It's a symbol of our family—a symbol of where we belong."

"Camila's mother thinks her father should have it."

Arturo's brow darkened. "Because he is head of the family. It's true; he has the right to it."

"But you won't give it to him."

"It belongs in Mexico. Just like my uncle does. It's our shame he cannot be here."

"I'm not sure I understand."

Arturo gave him a long look. "Our story isn't unusual."

But still it took some prodding to get him to tell it.

In the end Arturo gave in. "My great-grandfather owned this ranch, but he made bad choices, and my grandfather made more bad choices. They got in debt. Too much debt. Used the ranch as security and couldn't make the payments. Had to hand the place over and still owed money. He was taken advantage of. Strong-armed into a loan with interest was so high he could never pay it back. Now we're tenants in our own home. We will never earn enough here to buy our land back. We can barely pay our rent and keep current with the loan. *Tío*

Diego sends us money every month from the earnings of his restaurant. That is why he and *Tía* Paula went to Houston in the first place. It breaks *Mamá*'s heart he has never made it back."

Carl thought it over as they returned to the house. Debt could break a family. The Torreses were hanging on, but he could see that beneath his good cheer, Arturo was a man who knew he didn't have a future.

Was there some way he could help?

Carl had made many contacts over the years, and he knew several businessmen in Mexico. When they went inside, he made his way to his room and was able to place a couple of calls before Camila knocked on his door to announce dinner was ready.

"Be there in a minute," he told her.

When he returned to the large kitchen, he got Arturo to one side.

"I need a guide to Acapulco. I need to attend to some business there. Think you could get away for a day or two? I'll foot the bill—I could really use some help."

"Sure thing." Arturo's face lit up at the thought of the adventure. "When?"

"Tonight. I'll have you back in forty-eight hours." He hated leaving Camila behind for that much time, but he didn't see another way around it. A phone conversation wouldn't be the same. He needed to meet Valenzuela face-to-face.

"I'll be ready."

Carl took his seat and glanced at Camila across the room, immediately noticing she didn't look happy. She stood by the stove with Ximena and Juana, her eyebrows knit together and her hands behind her back while her cousin and aunt ruled over the pots and pans, talking animatedly.

Carl wondered why Camila wasn't pitching in. He knew how much she loved to cook—especially dishes that honored her heritage. Now she hung back, uncertain.

Camila never looked uncertain in Chance Creek.

The pozole, when the women served it, turned out to be a hearty corn soup with avocado, lime, onion and an exhilarating blend of spices that warmed him to his core. Ximena served coffee with dinner, which he wasn't used to, but everyone else was drinking it so he didn't want to refuse, although he wondered if he'd be awake all night. Then she passed around a bottle of clear liquid.

"Mezcal," Arturo explained, clapping Carl on the back as he passed him the bottle. Carl was glad to see his driver wasn't drinking. He dubiously eyed the worm floating around in the clear liquid. Beside him, Camila raised her eyebrows and shook her head. Carl grinned. He'd been a rancher in Montana long enough to have tasted moonshine and other questionable spirits; he could handle mezcal.

He raised the bottle to his lips, took a gulp, then coughed and spluttered as it burned down his throat. Instead of fading, the burn just kept going and going, and everyone around the table exploded into laughter as he thumped his chest. He laughed, too, when he caught his breath and the tingling warmth spread through his body.

After dinner he caught a minute alone with Camila in the hall. She grinned at him. "Looks like you're having a good day."

"I am." Carl didn't know if it was the aftereffects of his long hours of work in the brilliant Mexican sun or some chemical reaction in the mixture of pozole, coffee and mezcal working its way into his system, but he felt good.

He wished he could invite Camila to Acapulco with them, but he figured that wouldn't fly. She was up to her eyes in family drama, and he had a feeling she'd want to stay here at her relatives' ranch until she sorted things out.

That was too bad—a couple of nights in luxury hotel in Acapulco with her sounded pretty good right about now—but on the positive side, it would give him the chance to confront Valenzuela before she realized what he was doing. He sensed Camila's family wouldn't like to be interfered with. But to Carl's way of thinking, even if Valenzuela owned the ranch fair and square, he was running down his own investment. Surely there was a way to make the man see that.

"I'll be fine here," Camila said when he told her he needed to head there to meet some business contacts. He didn't mention Valenzuela. "Can't say I'm getting anywhere with Juana," she went on, "but I think Ximena and I are making progress."

"Good." Waiting for the chance to be with Camila

was killing him. She was so close but so far away with everyone around them all the time. His hands ached to touch her. He wanted to draw her close and let her know how much he wanted her.

They were alone now. He leaned in for a kiss, but just as his mouth was about to capture hers, someone cleared their throat behind him, and Carl quickly stepped back, holding his hands up like he had a pistol pointed at him.

It was Arturo. "We'd better leave within the hour. As it is, we'll barely make Acapulco by midnight."

"I need to make a couple of phone calls. Then I'll be ready." He turned to Camila and saw his frustration echoed in her eyes. His body thrummed with wanting her, but as always, someone was watching. "Take care of yourself," he managed, his voice gruff with his unful-filled need. "I'll be back before you know it."

Camila sighed. "Have a good trip."

Olivia tried to steal our clock again, Maya texted first thing the next morning. *She and Noah got into a tug-of-war over it and nearly smashed it.*

Camila could only imagine that scene. *What happened?*

Liam came in, went for Olivia, somehow tripped and broke the coffee table. Olivia got away. Liam's even madder than before. He says Noah tripped him.

That doesn't seem likely, Camila wrote. *Gotta go. Talk later.* She was grateful she wasn't at the Flying W.

Not that things were much better at her aunt and

uncle's ranch, although when she arrived in the kitchen, for once Juana wasn't there. The room smelled great, and out of habit she moved to the sink, washed her hands and tied on an apron hanging from a nearby hook. Her father's birthday was in two days, and she still didn't have the mask to bring to him. Her mother had texted her this morning, wondering when she'd be home. *Still working on it,* Camila had texted back.

As if reading her mind, Ximena glanced over her shoulder from her station at the stove, smiled and said, "*Cariña*, can I ask you something?"

"Sure," Camila said and braced herself.

"You and your *papá* don't get along too well, do you?"

"Did he say that?" she asked carefully. She and her father had never gotten back on track after she'd moved away.

Ximena laughed. "Of course not. But you haven't said one word about little Dieguito since you got here, either."

Camila had never thought about her father as "little Dieguito." She knew Ximena and her father were twins, but she had a hard time wrapping her mind around the idea that anyone might get away with calling him a nickname. She could've believed he was a decade older than her aunt. Ximena was full of life, dressed head to toe in the latest fashions. Her father was world-weary, wrinkled... tired.

She blinked at her own realization. She'd figured that was just how fathers always looked, but now that she had Ximena to compare him to, she was shocked. He *was* tired, wasn't he?

Camila realized Ximena was waiting for a response. "We see things differently," she said.

Ximena laughed. "You've never spent time in Mexico City, correct?

Camila winced. Only in her lies.

"If you get the chance, go visit Bosque de Chapultepec. Biggest city park in the world, you know. A real forest. I paid a visit a few days ago. Been there a thousand times, and I always see something new that surprises me."

There was a forest in Mexico City? Camila was glad no one had ever pressed her for details about her supposed home country.

"Diego never shared my love for Chapultepec Forest. We went there once when we were young, oh, seventeen, eighteen, *no sé*. 'Gringos' was all he could say. I'd say, 'Look at the lake,' and he'd say, 'Look at the gringos.' 'Let's go the zoo!' 'Too many gringos.' Everywhere we went, rich tourists, speaking English, tongues tripping over all the indigenous words, complaining about the food and the air and the traffic. 'We'd do no better in their country,' I told him. 'Show some compassion.' He said, 'They shouldn't come here if they hate it so much. We never asked them to.' I had to keep him away from them or he would have given them all a piece of his mind. In the end he did—when we got to the castle."

"Castle?" Camila tried to picture that. She could picture her father lecturing strangers easily enough.

"There was a tour guide, see, a pretty little thing, probably her first real job out of high school. And there she was, Mexican through and through but speaking perfect English, leading a group of gringos around the castle. Before I could stop him, little Diego marches up and calls her out. Castillo Chapultepec was a place of heroic resistance against the American forces when they invaded us, you know. Diego told her as much, pointed out the statues of the *niños* heroes, the boy heroes, younger even than we were when they fought and died protecting their families. He told her that she should be ashamed for bringing tourists there. Poor girl, you could see she didn't know what to say to him. I felt so bad for her, I invited her to dinner with us. We became fast friends."

Camila had to laugh. She could just imagine that dinner. "Did *Papá* ever learn to get along with her?"

"I should hope so, seeing as he married her."

"He—" Camila blinked. "She was—"

"Paula Delfina Barrera Rosario."

Again, Camila was caught off guard. She'd never heard her mother call herself anything other than "Paula Torres." No one in the United States was that formal.

Ximena beamed and kissed Camila's cheek. "Diego loves his country, but he loves Paulita, too, and he loves you, *cariña*."

"He has an odd way of showing it." But Camila was glad Ximena had told the story because it forced her to see her father in a new light. He'd overcome his prejudices to move to the United States, where he could make a better life for his family. Camila knew that had been hard, even if she couldn't picture her father as a rancher.

"It's been hard for him to be away from his home," Ximena said, echoing her thoughts.

"Then why doesn't he move back?" Camila said lightly. It seemed to her he wanted it both ways—to escape his family's ranching background and at the same time be able to complain about his life in Houston.

"You really do not know?" Ximena pursed her lips when Camila shook her head. "*Ay, Cariña!* He is so stubborn, that one. Our family had fallen on hard times, you see. But Paula had relatives in Texas already. They helped your parents emigrate and start their business. Ever since, your parents have sent money back to the rest of us."

Papá had been sending money?

This was the first Camila had heard of it. She struggled to take it in. If he'd moved to Texas to make money—

Did that mean everything she'd assumed about her father was wrong?

Had he wanted to escape the ranch? Or had he loved it here and missed it terribly?

Ximena was still speaking. "I owe Diego everything, could never hope to pay him back. He sacrificed his own happiness so I wouldn't have to sacrifice mine. I married first, you see. And Gerardo and I had no connections across the border." Her shoulders lowered an inch. "I wish we could have done more."

"You have a ranch. Why do you need money?"

Camila was afraid her question was rude, but she needed to understand. Ximena explained how her family had come to lose ownership of the land and how they hoped—one day—to earn it back but that it seemed impossible.

Her words painted a whole new picture of Camila's father's life, and Camila ached with the knowledge of how unfair she'd been to him in her thoughts.

But he'd never told her any of this. Why hadn't he? She could have taken over the restaurant. Run the place herself. Her parents could have moved back, and she would have been the one to send money to support her family.

"*Cariña*, listen to me," Ximena said.

Camila tried to focus on her aunt, but it was hard. Her mind was spinning.

"I owe your father. I know that."

Camila nodded. "I'm sure he—"

"But I won't give him the mask."

The mask. Camila had almost forgotten all about it—forgotten her reason for coming here in the first place.

But she still couldn't afford to leave without it.

Not if she wanted to marry Carl.

Especially now that she knew why her mother wanted to give it to her father—to bring a little of Mexico to Houston for him since he couldn't go home.

"Why not?"

"Because I need it. I need it to lure him back here. *Cariña*, it's time, don't you see that?"

Camila was confused. "You want him home? But I thought… you just said… don't you need him to support you?"

There was pain in Ximena's dark eyes. "I should never have asked Dieguito to carry this burden for me for so long. It's too much to ask. When he left for Texas, we all assumed it would be temporary."

Camila nodded.

"I have three grown children. We can't be Diego's burden any longer. I'm too old to move across the border, and my boys are too involved in the ranch. But Juana—she's a woman now and an excellent cook. She's strong. She knows how to get things done. She can take over Diego's restaurant, and Diego—and all his children—can finally come home."

Camila stifled a disbelieving laugh. If her father would accept a woman at the helm, then she would be the one running his restaurant. But he wouldn't. He'd never even consider it—not even if it was *perfect Juana* asking—and she didn't think Mateo was interested enough to run the place on his own. As for her brothers and sisters, she doubted any of them wanted to move to Mexico. They were all established in Houston. They thought of themselves as Americans. Their children even more so. Just as Camila did.

Ximena sighed. "You're thinking your father is too stubborn to agree to such a plan, and you're right. This is why I must keep the mask. To force your mother's hand. She's the one who decreed they'd never come back across the border until they were coming home permanently. She'll come if she thinks I'll hand it over to Diego personally. I will tell her of the grand party we have planned already and ask them to join us."

Camila didn't know what to say. First of all, she didn't know if the plan would work. Second, if her parents moved to Mexico, where would that leave her family? It would split them—just like Ximena's family had been split.

Of course, she already lived a thousand miles from her parents. A flight from Houston to Taxco wasn't a big deal.

She wanted her parents to be happy.

But would her father ever agree to allow Juana to run his restaurant? She couldn't imagine that.

"Won't you miss Juana?" she managed to ask, imagining Christmas trips across the border.

Maybe that wouldn't be so bad…

"So much it will break my heart. But someday luck will smile on us again. We'll win back our ranch, and she'll come home. I know God can't want my family torn apart forever."

But Camila hardly heard her, for something else had occurred to her. No wonder her father had been so angry to find out Gerardo was sending her money when she moved to Montana. Camila gripped the counter. Had her uncle been sending the money her father sent to him? But why had he made the offer in the first place? Had he thought a girl wouldn't actually leave her family, move across the country and start her own restaurant? Camila was horrified at the thought of how carelessly she'd treated the arrangement. She'd been angry when her uncle hadn't followed through.

Now she was ashamed.

"Excuse me." She left the kitchen, too overwhelmed by this flood of new information to continue the conversation. She needed a moment alone to gather her thoughts. In the hall, she nearly crashed into Juana, who stood near the door, her face damp with tears.

Camila's stomach twisted. Had Juana heard everything they'd just said?

Did she think her mother was going to sacrifice her for her aunt and uncle's happiness?

Camila quickly tugged Juana down the hall to her cousin's room, meaning to assure her they would find another way, but as soon as the door was closed, Juana burst out, "Did you hear? *Mamá*—she said—she said she'd send me to Texas!"

"I won't let her do that," Camila rushed to say. "I'll be the one to take over my family's restaurant. It should be me—I'm the gringa, after all…"

She trailed off at the fury on Juana's face.

"You'll take over? You'll run the restaurant? You think you can take everything that's mine?"

"What?" Camila didn't understand. She tried again. "That's not what I meant at all! I thought you wanted to stay here with your family—I thought—"

"You never think of anyone but yourself! Camila the perfect American girl! Camila the restaurant owner!

Camila the star of the family!"

"That's not true!" Camila's voice rose. "You're the one who's always perfect. The one my father calls a saint. The real Mexican. The real cook. The one who steals my success no matter what I do. Go to Houston, then. You might as well—my father would much rather have you than me!"

She spun on her heel to retreat to her own room, but Juana pursued her. "Wait. Gringa, wait!"

Camila shook off her grasp. "For what? For you to tell me what a failure I am? Go on—everyone else has!"

"Failure?" Juana's eyes widened with shock. "Failure? What failure?"

Camila couldn't stand her pretense. "You know what failure. My failure to my family. My failure to my heritage. My failure to Mexico!"

"But…" Juana touched her arm again. "Who said this?"

"You did!" Camila exploded. All she wanted was to escape. The walls of her aunt's house, so welcoming, now felt like they were closing in on her. Her parents felt the same way Juana did. No matter what she accomplished, it would never be enough.

Juana stared at her, then took hold of her arm. "Come!" She tugged her back into the room.

Camila allowed herself to be dragged along. Why not get it over with, whatever Juana had in mind? Her cousin had hated her on sight. She probably had something to show her that would prove once and for all that she belonged—that she was a true Torres—

while Camila was—

Nothing.

Juana closed and locked her door before kneeling to open the bottom drawer of her dresser. Under a layer of clothes, she pulled out several objects—a rolled up poster, a few old CDs.

Juana unrolled the poster and showed Camila.

Camila blinked. "Is that... Shakira?"

Juana nodded and showed her another, this one of Diego Luna. All in all, she had an impressive set of pop culture memorabilia—all with a Mexican connection, but all of it distinctly American.

"I always wanted to go to the Estados Unidos," Juana explained. "To see Hollywood, New York City, all of it. It's my dream. But to hear *Mamá* speak of *Tío* Diego and the choice he made—it's like he chose death over life. I've always felt if I followed my dream—to join him—to run my own restaurant in Houston—I would be betraying her. But now she wants me to go!"

"Oh, Juana." Camila remembered how her cousin had reacted to the photo of Fila's. It must have seemed like she was taunting Juana. Proving she had everything her cousin always wanted. No wonder Juana had taken every chance to belittle her cooking.

Camila wasn't sure whether to laugh or cry. Did Juana really think *she* was the paragon?

Hardly.

"Is that what you want? To go to Houston?"

"To America, *sí*. I have my visa. I hoped to go to visit first and find someone to sponsor me for a job. I thought *Mamá* would never agree—but now I don't have to break her heart!" Juana's eyes shone. "But your father…" She broke off and rolled her eyes. "I listen to *Mamá*'s conversations. I hear what she says and what she doesn't say when she speaks to him. I know how it is. He is…" She waved a hand. "How do you say it? Old-fashioned. He doesn't think women can run anything. And your brother—he sounds the same. *Mi chiquita cocinera*, that's what he calls me when we speak. Like I'm some child playing in the kitchen, not a chef to be taken seriously." She made a dismissive noise. "I know what will happen. If *Tío* Diego comes here to live, he'll demand that Mateo stay in Houston and be the boss. I can't work for him—I won't work for him. I am just as good as any man. Better." She lifted her chin. "So now I have a different plan. And it involves you."

She looked at Camila, and her eyes were filled with so much hope it took Camila's breath away. "Could I come to Montana and… work for you?"

CARL'S MEXICAN CONTACTS had proven very useful, and a few promises had secured him an invitation to a party tonight Valenzuela planned to attend. After a day exploring Acapulco's shops and beaches, and several hours in which Carl and Sven updated each other on their progress with the school proposal and brainstormed the best way to present their project to the school board, he and Arturo arrived to find the event in full swing. Arturo, already nervous, let out huff of surprise when they were shown to a rooftop patio. Carl understood why. The decor was as breathtaking as anything he'd seen during his many years in business. Hundreds of fairy lights lit the patio, the buffet tables groaned with finger foods and drinks, and a crowd of revelers dressed to the nines talked, laughed and danced to a live DJ's mix.

Carl was too busy looking for Valenzuela to appreciate the venue for long, though. He had business to take care of—and Camila to get back to. When he spotted Valenzuela in the crowd, he steered Arturo to a spot by the buffet table.

"I'll be back soon," he told him. He'd kept the details of his plan to himself, only telling Arturo he needed to meet someone, partly because he didn't know how Arturo would feel about his meddling and partly because he had no idea how he was going to play this himself.

"Don't be too long." Arturo clearly felt out of place. He eased into a position near the wall, eyeing the food and the crowd in the same suspicious manner.

Carl remembered his first time at an important party like this. He'd been no more comfortable than Arturo was. Making a promise to himself he'd be as quick as he could, he crossed to where Valenzuela stood chatting with a small knot of guests.

Domingo Valenzuela was shorter than Carl had imagined, with a round red face and a round body to match. He had a hearty laugh, but Carl noticed his gaze swept the party constantly, as if the man didn't want to miss out on any action. While Arturo had been intimidated by the other guests, Carl wasn't cowed by the thought of confronting Valenzuela. He had no respect for a man who had brought so much misery to Camila's family.

In his own business dealings, Carl had always walked the line between pushing his employees and reigning them in. He'd tried to inspire those who worked beneath him, rather than act like an absentee landlord determined to scrape the last dime from his tenants before the house collapsed around them all.

Carl figured Valenzuela would keep the pressure on Camila's family until something broke—until the ranch fell to pieces due to lack of repairs, or someone was hurt, or the herd was left unprotected from the elements. He'd seen signs of ill-repair on some of the outbuildings already, and he had no doubt the Torres' budget didn't run to making them whole again.

A fool, that's what this man was. A fool who didn't know something good when he had it in his hand. The Torreses would work heart and soul to make the ranch profitable if they could. It was only the unfair terms of their loan that were dragging them down.

Valenzuela met his gaze several times, and when he realized Carl was waiting to speak to him, detached himself from the other guests and came his way. *"Bienvenido, mi amigo, mucho gusto.* I do not think that we have met. Juan Manuel Domingo Valenzuela de la Cruz, at your service—but you may call me Domingo."

Good thing. Carl hadn't caught half those names. He accepted the offered hand. "Whitfield. Carl Whitfield."

"You aren't from around here, I think."

"Just down from Montana," Carl told him.

"What brings you to the most beautiful country in the world?" Valenzuela asked.

"The most beautiful woman in the world."

Valenzuela chuckled. "That explains it. What is she like?"

Carl had meant to get straight to the accusations he'd come here to make, but he found himself saying, "She's really something. Smart, stubborn, a little fiery. A self-made entrepreneur. Started with nothing and built a very popular and successful restaurant."

"Our country does breed exceptional women."

Carl frowned. "She isn't from Mexico, actually." Of course, she didn't know he knew that. Sooner or later they'd have to have that conversation. "Which is why I'm here. Her people are from Taxco. Her father was forced to move to America to escape poverty. We're here visiting her Mexican relatives, who still depend on him to send money back to them every month."

Valenzuela's eyes shone with sympathy. "*Ay,* a sad tale. Tell me of their situation. How did it come to this?"

Carl told him the story as he'd gleaned it from Arturo. How Camila's family had bought their ranch, then fallen into debt over the years. How that debt had snowballed until suddenly their property wasn't their property anymore. How they had no way of getting out from under it now and paid such high interest on their loan they couldn't keep up with rent and repairs.

How the ranch's owner didn't seem to care.

"A sorry situation," Valenzuela agreed. "A poor businessman, this owner, in addition to being a cruel and apathetic man. Do you know his name, by any chance? I have many connections, especially in Guerrero. Perhaps I can talk some sense into this poor deluded man."

Carl met his gaze. "His name is Domingo Valenzuela."

CAMILA SURGED AWAKE early the next morning when someone pounded on her bedroom door. Her heart in her mouth, she leaped from her bed and grabbed her robe, but she only had it halfway on when Juana burst into the room.

"They're coming! They said yes!"

"Who said yes?"

"*Tío* Diego and *Tía* Paula. *Mamá* was so happy when they agreed! I'm not sure your *mamá* was as pleased." Juana laughed. "But when *Mamá* told her she'd hand over the mask, she agreed to cross the border for the first time since she left. They will arrive tomorrow morning. We have so much to do! Luckily, everyone has already been invited to my mother's party. We will have a wonderful surprise for them when your parents show up!"

Camila caught her breath. Juana was right; they had a lot to do. She was impressed Ximena had managed to force her mother's hand. But then, she was right—it was her mother, not her father, who had the rule about not visiting Mexico until they moved back permanently. She was sure if her mother had agreed to come for the party, her father wouldn't have objected.

He was probably thrilled.

Camila hoped it cheered him up, even if the rest of the plan didn't work. Her father had seemed so worn down when she saw him in Texas.

"Come quickly. We need to start cooking!"

Juana wasn't kidding. Camila spent the rest of the day with her aunt and cousin in the kitchen, preparing for the big celebration. At first she hung back the way she had since she'd arrived, afraid to make mistakes, but Juana put her to work. She still hadn't apologized for her previous bad behavior, but she seemed determined to make up for it. She praised everything Camila did to the skies and had taken to calling her *Cocinera* Camila, with an impish grin that made Camila smile in return. Camila decided that if their positions were switched, she would have been pretty cranky, too. Now that Juana knew she had an adventure ahead of her she was a changed woman. She danced around the kitchen, helping Ximena and Camila, cracking jokes and doing impressions of her family members that left Camila in stitches.

Thank goodness for Ximena's plan. It would have been a shame not to get to know this side of her cousin. Camila was beginning to think Juana could be that long-lost sister she'd always hoped for.

Camila texted Carl to let him know her parents were

coming and to tell him about the preparations they were making for her father and Ximena's birthday party. When he texted back to say he was on his way to the ranch right now, she realized how much she'd missed him. She was enjoying her time with Ximena and Juana today, but it wasn't the same as being with him.

She helped make *tamales oaxaqueños, chilaquiles verdes*, tacos and a number of salsas: *pico de gaillo, salsa verde,* guacamole and a *salsa roja* so spicy it burned Camila's eyes when she sniffed it. Then there were dishes that were less familiar to Camila: *esquites*, a creamy, soupy dish of corn and cheese and mayonnaise, flavored with lime, powdered *piquín* peppers and *epazote*, an herb that was hard to find north of the border; and *molletes*, long slices of bread topped with refried beans and melted cheese. At least dessert was familiar: flan, a universal favorite.

Working with her aunt and cousin gave Camila the opportunity to learn a lot more about her family. It turned out her paternal grandparents had come from two completely different lineages. Her father's mother had roots in Taxco that could be traced back to the Aztec Empire. Her father's father came from a more scattered ancestry and had relatives from Guatemala to New Mexico. Her father clearly took after his mother, while Ximena took after her father. She frequently traveled back and forth between the ranch and Mexico City, maintaining strong ties with both the provincial and metropolitan sides of her family. That detail gave Camila some hope that maybe the estranged elements of their family could come back together, after all.

Camila realized how comfortable she'd become here, more comfortable than she'd felt for years with her own family in America. Juana was proving to be fun. And Ximena was becoming as dear to her as her own mother.

"So," Ximena began that afternoon when they were alone in the kitchen. "This Carl. Is he the one?"

"I think so," Camila said.

"Do you want to marry? To have kids?"

"Yes. Someday."

Ximena pursed her lips. "I think your man's in a bigger hurry than you are."

"He said that?"

"He didn't have to. I can see it in him. Think carefully about your future. I think it's coming sooner than you might guess."

Maybe, Camila thought darkly. But not if they never even managed to make out.

Chapter Six

AS ARTURO TURNED the truck onto the long, winding dirt road that wound up the hill to the Torres family ranch, Carl's phone began to buzz. He checked the screen, and when he found it was Virginia calling, he reluctantly answered.

"What is it, Virginia?"

"Where's my presentation?"

Carl sighed. "I've pulled a lot of it together," he assured her, "but I'll need to work with your architect to finalize it."

"Then you'd better get back here—today!"

"I can't come today. But I promise I'll be there in time to get the presentation done."

"I'm beginning to think your promises are worth less than the paper they're written on."

"I haven't written them on any paper," Carl pointed out.

"Exactly."

"Virginia, I'll be there as soon as I possibly can."

"No presentation, no ranch," she reminded him.

"Believe me; I know." Carl hung up. He was glad Camila's father was coming tomorrow and that Ximena had agreed to give him the mask. Carl needed to leave tomorrow right after the party, make a quick trip back to Chance Creek, soothe Virginia's ruffled feathers, talk to her architect and then hightail it out to California.

"When are we going to tell them the good news?" Arturo asked when he pulled up to the house and killed the truck's engine.

"Tomorrow, when everyone's here. Can you keep the secret overnight?"

"Of course. They'll be so surprised."

After Carl had leveled his accusations at Valenzuela last night, the man had consented to sit down with him and Arturo. They'd ended up being some of the last guests to leave the party after talking long into the evening, Carl mediating while the two men explained their perspectives.

He and Arturo had learned the ranch had been an acquisition early in Valenzuela's career, before he'd moved out of agriculture and focused his business more squarely in the energy sector. The ranches that Valenzuela still technically owned were now under the management of one of his partners. He'd admitted, with some embarrassment, he had no idea he even still owned the Torres ranch.

Carl had been indignant until he realized he often stretched himself just as thin, meddling in affairs all the way from Silicon Valley to Acapulco.

Once they were all three on the same page, they'd put their heads together to come up with a new plan. Carl hoped the rest of the family would like it.

"Thanks for all your help," he told Arturo, dropped his bag in his room and made a beeline for the kitchen, where he suspected he'd find Camila. Her face lit up when she saw him, and a weight slipped off his shoulders. His trip had been worth it if it made her life better.

"*Hola,*" she said.

"*Hola.*" He cleared his throat, finding it difficult to go on. He'd meant to simply say hello and make sure things were okay with her, but now that they were close, he wanted much more than that. He moved closer, waited until Ximena was busy stirring something in a pan and whispered, "Meet me out back in five minutes."

"But—"

"Five minutes," he repeated and escaped out the door again. He'd had enough of waiting. Tomorrow Camila's extended family would arrive, including her parents. Who knew when he'd get this chance again.

He had the horses ready by the time she slipped outside.

"I told Ximena I'd be back in a few minutes," she said, eyeing them askance.

Carl didn't answer. Instead he laced his fingers together, held them out for her to step on and lifted her into the saddle of a midnight-black mare.

"I mean it," she said again when they set off down the hill. "I can't be gone long."

"I'll get you back soon enough."

Just as soon as he'd claimed that kiss circumstances kept denying him.

WHY HADN'T SHE done this sooner?

Camila followed Carl down the side of a hill, the wind whipping her curls behind. She relished the fresh air and motion after the hours she'd spent in Ximena's kitchen. They slowed when they approached the woods, picking their way along a narrow winding trail. After the constant bustle of the ranch house, the quiet of the forest calmed her. When they reached a river, Carl dismounted and helped Camila down, too.

She thought he'd kiss her then, but instead he sat down, slid off his boots and dipped his feet in the cool water. Camila followed suit and moaned with pleasure. It was beautiful here, birds chirping overhead as the water slid by. When Carl touched the back of her hand, she turned to him, taking in his grave expression.

"I want to be with you, Camila," he said. "You know that, right?"

She nodded.

"I had a meeting with someone important yesterday," he went on. "And that's a problem."

"Why?"

"Because every meeting feels important. There's always another deal. Another problem to solve. Another old friend who needs me."

"I understand; that's who you are. A businessman."

He lightly bumped her shoulder with his. "But you don't want to be with a businessman. You want a rancher. Someone who stays in Chance Creek."

Camila sucked in a breath. "That's not fair. I'm not trying to dictate your job. I simply want assurances I won't have to move." If only he could see inside her heart. Know how much she loved him even if she was terrified that doing so meant she'd someday have to leave Chance Creek.

"I get that." Carl took a moment to find his words. "And I am going to be a rancher in Chance Creek, one way or another."

One way or another? Camila realized he'd never updated her on his progress buying the Simmons's ranch. Was he worried the deal would fall through?

"But I'm always going to be a businessman, too. A ranch is a business, and I'm always going to be looking for ways to improve our cattle operation. That's who I am. That's what interests me. I want to put you first, but my business life is going to intrude sometimes. How do you feel about that?"

Camila leaned back, resting her weight on her wrists. How *did* she feel about that? She knew how important it was to her to be with Carl, but she also worried his love of business would one day lead him away from Chance Creek.

When her silence went on too long, Carl touched her knee. "Let me put it another way. How do you want to spend *your* time?"

"Running my restaurant," she said immediately.

"Is there anything else you want to do?"

She laughed. There was hardly enough time in the day already.

"Will you cut back your hours so you're home for dinner every night if we marry?" he asked.

Camila straightened. "How could I possibly do that? Dinner is our busiest time."

"But you'll take weekends off?"

She doubted it. "I take Mondays off."

"But if I need you, I can call you up and you'll come right home?"

"Carl!" She knew what he was doing. Knew it was only fair. But still—

He raised an eyebrow but didn't say anything more. He was an exasperating man sometimes. A sexy, exasperating man.

She forced herself to think the situation through. They were both busy people, and their schedules were never going to be consistent. And just when they'd found a ranch, she'd been the one to send them on a wild goose chase to Texas—and then Mexico.

"I've been asking for the moon, huh?" she asked. "I've been making this impossible."

"No. Not impossible. But hard." Carl picked up a stone and tossed it in his hand. "I'm wondering if there's another reason—besides wanting to be sure you get to stay in Chance Creek."

"Another reason?"

"For setting the bar to date you so high. Maybe I'm not really the man you want."

Camila turned on him. "Carl Whitfield, I want you," she told him, "so just shut your stupid mouth." She flushed when she realized what she'd said, but Carl only chuckled.

"Glad to hear it." He grew serious again. "Maybe it's

something else, then. Maybe you're not ready to marry."

Camila opened her mouth to deny it, but nothing came out.

Carl shifted. "We don't have to rush things, you know." But she could tell he wished she'd answered differently. Camila let the water run over her feet and tried to put her thoughts in order.

"I think—I think you're right," she said slowly. "I wasn't ready for a serious relationship—or marriage—the first time we went out. Don't get me wrong," she added quickly. "I'd already fallen for you back then. Hard. But we went straight from nothing to everything. We talked about marriage on our first date!"

"And we're doing it again," he said ruefully. "I asked you to say yes to a ranch—as if you'd already said yes to me."

"We can't hide how we feel about each other," Camila said. "We just… *work* together. But back then…"

"Back then?" he prompted when she didn't go on.

"Back then I was just getting started at Fila's. I'd always worked for my father. Lived with my parents. Got bossed around by my older brother. For the first time I was getting to run my own life. You're older than me, Carl. You're already a successful businessman. It would have been way too easy to slide right back into an old pattern and let you take the lead. That's not what I wanted. I still don't want that."

He cocked his hat back. "I thought it might be something like that."

"Are you angry?"

"No. I get it, actually. As a young man, I had to move away from home to take control of my life; otherwise I'd have looked to my father to make the decisions. You needed to find your feet."

"Exactly."

"How about now?" Carl asked, tossing the stone in his hand again.

"Now I think I'm ready. Although I'd still like a date or two before we get any more serious."

"Doesn't this count as a date?"

"I guess so." She made a face. How much of a date could it be if they didn't even kiss?

Carl must have read her mind. He reached for her—

But the sound of hoofbeats had him scrambling back.

"Carl? Camila?" Luis called as he reined in his horse. "You're needed up at the house."

Chapter Seven

"WHY HASN'T HE sent the offer?" Sven asked for the tenth time that evening.

"Because he's trying to throw you off," Carl said. He leaned back on his bed in the guest room and watched the sun disappearing below the horizon. "Fulsom knows you're new at this, and he knows how badly you want his offer. He's got all the power, and he's letting you know that. We've been over this." It was a struggle to keep calm enough to soothe his friend; he was consumed with thoughts of Camila after Luis had interrupted them earlier. At least the man hadn't caught them going at it right there on the creek bed. Ten more minutes and he would have.

"But he said he'd send it in a couple of days. He said he wanted this all wrapped up by the tenth."

"Then expect the offer on the ninth."

"Would he really do that?"

Carl could picture his friend pacing his office. Sven sounded frantic. He felt for the man, but of the two of them he thought he was more deserving of pity. He'd waited three years for the chance to be with Camila. Just as he'd been about to buy a ranch, it was stolen out from under him. Now he was thrown together with her night and day and he wasn't even allowed to kiss her, let alone everything else he wanted to do with her. And who knew if Virginia even had a ranch to point him to when all was said and done with the school project.

"He might. Look. There's nothing more you can do right now. You're ready for the deal when it comes. Take tonight off. Go see a movie. Do something."

"But you'll be here in two days no matter what?"

"Yes. As soon as the party is over tomorrow I'll fly back to Chance Creek. Meet the architect the next morning, and be on a plane to California that evening."

"I feel like I'm losing my mind," Sven told him.

I know what you mean, Carl wanted to tell him. Instead he said, "Go to the gym. Or go for a jog. Don't let Fulsom get to you."

"I guess I can do that."

"You'll feel a lot better. Get all that adrenaline out of your system, then go home and go to bed. Be fresh for tomorrow."

"What if the deal comes while I'm sleeping?" Sven asked.

"It won't." Not if he knew Fulsom.

Carl called Virginia next, but to his surprise Olivia picked up.

"Virginia's phone," she chirped.

"Olivia? What are you doing?" He climbed off the bed and crossed the floor, straightened a few knick-knacks on the bureau and crossed the room the other way to gaze out the window. Great; now he was the one pacing.

"I'm supposed to tell her when you call. She's taking an after-dinner nap."

"Virginia naps?"

Olivia laughed. "Don't ever tell her I told you."

"Things going all right there?"

"If you're asking if we've had another pitched battle with the Turners lately, the answer is no."

"Good to hear."

"It's getting a little boring."

"Please don't spice things up."

Olivia laughed again. "You're a stick-in-the-mud. Let me get my aunt."

"Wait—" Carl held his breath until Olivia came back on the line.

"What?"

"Don't wake her. Just tell her I'm on it and I'll be home soon."

"She won't believe you."

"Tell her anyway."

Done with his phone calls, Carl spent what was left of the evening helping set up for the party the following day. The women had decorated the house with candles and garlands, and he was beginning to look forward to the festivities.

Whenever his gaze met Arturo's, the other man's eyes glinted with their shared secret. He knew Camila's cousin was dying to let the cat out of the bag.

Carl managed to get a moment alone with Camila late that night. "Ready for tomorrow?"

"I think so. You?"

"Sure, but it's not my rodeo." He put his hands on her hips. "I want to be with you," he growled.

"I know. It's like being a teenager." Her fingers tightened on his shoulders where they rested. Then she let go, smoothed the fabric of his shirt and sighed. "I don't know what my parents will think about Ximena's idea when they get here. And I don't know what Ximena is going to think when she realizes Juana has a different plan."

"I guess we'll see what happens when it happens. Camila—" He tugged her close before rapid footsteps approaching in the corridor sent him backpedaling toward his room. Camila darted toward hers.

"Good night," she whispered from her doorway, grinning mischievously at him.

"Good night." When she'd slipped into her room, Carl entered his own, shut his door with a click and had to laugh. Camila was right; it was like being teenagers.

And he was ready to be a grown up with Camila.

WHEN CAMILA'S PHONE buzzed early the next morning, she nearly didn't answer it, but when she saw her brother's name on the screen she slipped out of the busy kitchen and into the yard to take it in private.

"Mateo? Is something wrong?"

"Did *Tía* Ximena give *Papá* the mask yet?"

"No. They haven't even arrived yet. The party starts at lunchtime. What's going on?"

"It's just… he's miserable, Camila. And so am I. I

don't know what to do."

Camila was surprised he was confessing this to her. She and her brother hadn't had a real talk in ages. "Can you keep a secret?" she asked.

"Of course."

She wasn't sure he could, but her parents were due any minute. He wouldn't have time to warn their father about the trap Ximena had set for him. "*Tia* Ximena had an idea," she said and explained all about the mask and her plan to send Juana across the border.

"So Juana's going to run the restaurant?"

She could hear Mateo bristling at the idea. "Actually, no, but Ximena doesn't know that yet. Juana doesn't want to work with you; she wants to work with me. She can send money home from Montana as easily as from Texas."

"So… I'll run the restaurant by myself?" He didn't sound as pleased as she thought he might be.

"Don't you want to?"

"I don't even like cooking that much," he said. "Now it'll all be on me."

Camila held the phone away from her ear for a moment. A fine time for Mateo to admit what she'd always suspected. Why did he make such a fuss about being in control if he didn't even like the job?

"What do you want to do?" she asked when she pressed the phone against her ear again.

"Something else."

"Then I think you'd better tell *Papá* that," she said in exasperation. "After his birthday party. Let's see what he chooses to do first."

"Fine. Talk to you later."

"Mateo?" she said, worried by how discouraged he sounded.

"Yeah?"

"I miss you."

Her brother sighed. "Miss you, too." He hung up.

"DIEGO! MY BROTHER," Ximena cried when Camila's parents arrived later that morning. She threw her arms around Camila's father and gave him a bear hug. Carl hung back as the family exchanged greetings and were ushered into the kitchen. "It's been so long." Ximena hugged Diego again, tears gathering in the corners of her eyes. "I thought you might never come home."

Camila was watching her parents anxiously, and Carl had braced for discord between Ximena and Paula, but Camila's mother had stopped near the table and stood looking around as if trying to memorize every inch of the room. She inhaled deeply. "It smells like home." Her eyes were moist, too.

Even Diego looked like a man close to tears.

Carl wondered if he should give the family some space, but when he stepped toward the door, Ximena swooped across the room and took his arm. "We have so enjoyed getting to know Carl," she said. "He is a wonderful man. And your daughter—she is wonderful, too. Her cooking—amazing!"

Diego lifted his gaze in surprise at that, and Carl was glad Ximena had said so. Camila never got enough praise from her family.

"She takes after her father. We are proud of her," Paula said.

Camila's eyebrows shot up, and Carl had to hold back a laugh. Funny how family never said anything nice to your face but bragged about you to everyone else.

"Come. Sit. Our other guests will arrive in an hour, but for now it is just family. I will get you something to drink."

Soon they were all seated around the table, except for Ximena and Juana, who kept working on the meal they were preparing for the party.

Carl noticed Diego looking at the empty shelf where the mask usually presided over the room.

Diego frowned. "You moved the mask?"

"Let's talk about that later," Ximena said from the stove.

"I would like to see it after all these years. Where is it?"

"First you need to rest, brother. Here, have some coffee. Take a breath." She handed out cups of the strong brew to everyone.

"Where have you put it?"

Ximena looked to Paula in desperation. Paula shrugged. "You might as well give it to him now. It's why we're here, after all."

"Yes, it's why you're here. But it is a complicated conversation and—"

"Complicated? How?" Paula demanded. "Are you going back on your word?" She set her coffee cup down on its saucer with a thump.

"Of course not."

"Then what is there to talk about?"

"Where the mask will stay." Ximena put her hands on her hips.

"It will stay with Diego," Paula said. Diego looked from one to the other as if he was watching a ping-pong match.

"Exactly, which means Diego must stay here. In Mexico!" Ximena burst out.

Paula couldn't seem to find an answer to that. "Stay here?" she finally managed.

"You know I'd like that, Ximena," Diego said wearily. "And you know why I can't. Let's not discuss it. As for the mask, it is generous of you to offer it as a present, but it must stay here, where the heart of our family is."

"You are the heart of the family, *hermanito*," Ximena said, bustling over to the table. "We need you here, too. With the mask. My daughter—my Juana—is ready to go to Texas and work in your place. It is time for the next generation to take up the burden."

"Juana?" Diego's chin went up. "She is a girl."

"*Mamá*, I don't want to go to Texas!" Juana said hurriedly. "I want—"

Ximena shushed her. "That's enough, *cariña*. It is all agreed."

"It's not agreed." Diego slapped a hand on the table. "I have a daughter myself. I don't need daughters. I need to keep this family afloat. That is a man's job. I will do it. End of conversation."

Ximena threw her hands in the air. "You are being ridiculous. I'm solving everything—"

"Not everything—" Juana said angrily.

"Hush." Ximena turned back to Diego. "Why won't you listen to me? Juana is a good worker. Smart. Strong."

"I say it again—it takes a man to run a restaurant."

"Then why don't you let Mateo run it by himself?" Camila burst out angrily. Carl couldn't blame her for being angry at her father's blanket put-down of women.

Paula and Diego both looked away. Carl wondered why. Did they worry Mateo couldn't run it alone?

Or did they want to stay in Texas?

Diego's shoulders sagged suddenly. "Mateo is a fine son," he said, "but you know the restaurant business… sometimes his heart, it isn't in it." The admission seemed to take all the air out of his lungs, and Carl felt for the man, forced to admit his son's failings in front of everyone.

Camila stood up, pushing her chair back so abruptly it scraped over the slate floor. "Right. Even he's admitted that now. And yet you let me go to Montana rather than embarrass him. When my heart *is* in my cooking."

"You don't understand a man's pride, Camila," Diego told her. "You never have. You don't understand what it would do to a first son to be pushed aside by a daughter."

"I might not understand a man's pride," Camila said tightly. "But I know exactly what it does to a daughter to be kicked out of her own home so that a son can keep his!" She crossed her arms over her chest. "Now you're making Mateo miserable by forcing him to do a job he doesn't even like."

"Which is why I must stay. To make sure the job is done right," Diego asserted.

Ximena spoke up again. "Juana will solve this problem. She will make sure the job is done right."

"What if I don't want to? What if Mateo doesn't want my help?" Juana crossed her arms, too. "*Dios*, you two really are twins, aren't you? Always thinking you know what's best for everybody else." She looked from Ximena to Diego. "I barely know my cousin, and yet it's clear as day he wasn't meant to run a restaurant. But you two won't even ask what he wants to do. I know how that feels. I've spent my life pretending I didn't want to visit *Tío* Diego and *Tía* Paula. That I didn't want to travel and learn about new things. Well, guess what? That's exactly what I want to do—and I'm not going to let you use me to make Mateo feel even worse! I'm going to Montana with Camila. The rest of you can stay here and fight over that stupid mask like dogs over a scrap of meat."

"Montana? But—" Ximena stared at her daughter, clearly at a loss.

Diego shook his head. "That settles it. If she goes to Montana, I stay in Houston."

Paula lifted her hands. "Maybe we should sell the restaurant and help buy back this ranch."

Diego turned on her. "This again! If we do that,

what legacy can we hand to Mateo—and our other children? They are not ranchers. They don't want to move back here. They are Americans now."

"I just said I'll send home the money I earn in Montana," Juana burst out. "Why isn't anyone listening to me?"

"Because without help, Mateo will fail," Diego said. "I will not allow that, either."

"You are so stubborn!" Paula lit into him. Juana joined her, and soon the noise level rose as everyone competed to be heard.

"I will keep working for my family, like I've always done. Mateo—"

"Mateo knows nothing of cooking," Paula shouted at Diego. "All he knows is that stupid music! Blasting it night and day—"

Camila straightened, and Carl leaned forward. He could tell she'd had an idea. But she'd be hard-pressed to make herself heard over the shouting. He figured her family was far more likely to listen if a stranger interrupted them.

"Camila?" he said loudly. "What do you think?"

Just as he'd anticipated, the room fell silent as the whole family turned to look first at him, then at her.

"I think there's an answer no one's considered yet," she said slowly.

CAMILA WAITED UNTIL a new spate of exclamations died down before speaking again. Her mother was right; Mateo could care less about Mexican food, but if there was a new band within five-hundred miles, you could bet he'd try to score a ticket. He made friends with everyone he could in the music business. Was constantly inviting bands back to the restaurant to eat.

"What if you let Mateo do what he really wants to do? Turn the restaurant into a club—and book live music? It could be a real money earner."

Diego looked indignant, but Paula stared at her. "*Ay, Dios.* She's right." Suddenly, she smiled. "Camila is right. Why have we never thought of that? He could do it, Diego."

"But my restaurant—"

"Could still be a restaurant," Camila told him. "It would simply feature music and dancing, too. Mateo would be the manager. He could hire someone to run the food side of the business."

Carl nodded at her, and Camila's spirits rose. It was a good idea, and she could see her brother working night and day to make it successful.

"It would make our son happy," her mother said to her father. "Think about it, *gordito.*"

"*Sí,*" he said slowly. "You're right; it would."

"I'll still send money back as long as you need it, to help things out," Juana added eagerly.

Ximena nodded. She turned to Diego. "And you will help us do everything we can to increase our income here. We don't want to be a burden on our children forever."

"All of us working together will pay off the debt in no time," Juana said happily.

Camila didn't correct her, but she knew that wasn't quite accurate. With the changes Mateo would have to make to the restaurant, it would be some time before he could send much money here, but with all of them focusing on it, they could get it done. She'd never even known about these debts. She bet none of her siblings did, either. If everyone helped a little, surely they could get the situation in hand.

"So?" Ximena asked Camila's parents. "You'll come home? We'll be together?"

"Yes," Paula said emphatically. She nudged Diego. "Tell her it is so."

"We must talk to Mateo first and listen to his answer," Diego said. "But if he agrees, then… yes. Yes, I think we could move home. If we all work hard, one day we may pay off our debts."

Arturo snorted. "*Dios mío*, Carl, when can we tell them our news?"

Camila turned to Carl in surprise.

Carl chuckled. "I guess now is as good a time as any."

"I KNOW I said I went to Acapulco to meet with an associate," Carl began. "That wasn't entirely true. I met with Señor Valenzuela, and he's agreed to make some modifications to your agreement. He had passed the ranch on to a partner to manage, and he was disappointed to learn how the man had taken advantage of the situation. We went over the numbers, and I was able to prove that you've been paying far more interest than you should have for years. Valenzuela agreed to write down the debt considerably. From now on a portion of your monthly payment will go toward the purchase of the property."

"That's not all," Arturo chimed in. "Valenzuela agreed to match any money we put into repairs or upgrades for the ranch."

Carl nodded. "With another provision that these upgrades will not be counted toward the ranch's value regarding your purchase of the property. You only have to pay off the ranch's current value. A man should be by sometime this week to make a final appraisal, and then you'll receive a new contract, but I think you'll find the terms more than reasonable."

Diego turned to Camila. "Is this true?"

She kept her gaze on Carl. "It's the first I've heard of it. But if Carl says it's true, then it is. You can trust him."

Relief filled Carl. She wasn't angry he'd interfered.

Instead she'd sounded... proud.

But Carl didn't want this day to be about him, so he was glad when a knock on the front door announced the first of their guests. As he stood up with the others to greet them, Camila came and took his arm.

"Thank you," she said. "You don't know how grateful I am. This debt seems like it's been a millstone around my family's neck; I had no idea how much it was dragging everyone down. How long will it take to pay it off, do you think?"

"A while," he cautioned her, "but the way the loan

was arranged before, they'd never have paid it off—and never gotten to buy the ranch back, either." He hesitated. "You know I'd gladly contribute—"

She shook her head. "You have contributed, in a way that allows my family to keep its honor. You can't be the one to pay it off. We have to do that."

"I had a feeling you'd say that."

"You've done more than you know."

"What do you mean?"

She smiled impishly. "*Mamá* said she wouldn't give me permission to marry you until the mask was in my father's hands." She nodded to where Ximena had just placed a wrapped package on the table in front of him.

"You should have told me!" Carl tugged her closer. "What if I'd lost you?"

"*Dios mio*, the way you two behave."

When Carl pulled back, he found Paula shaking her head at him. But then she smiled, and he knew he really did have her blessing to court Camila.

LATER THAT AFTERNOON Carl was in the kitchen by himself when Diego wandered in, saw him, nodded, poured himself a cup of coffee and joined Carl at the table. The rest of the party had moved into the living room after they'd eaten their fill, and now the house hummed with the low murmur of conversation, the guests mellow from good food and drink. Carl was working out his flights home. The next forty-eight hours were going to be busy.

"So, you talked to Valenzuela," Diego said.

"Yes."

"Money has its perks."

Carl couldn't argue with that. "Yes. Connections, too."

"I suppose I need to thank you." Diego didn't sound too eager to do that, but Carl understood he was a proud man.

"No thanks needed. But I did want to have a word with you. About Camila."

"You want permission to marry her."

"Yes." Carl didn't feel the need to elaborate. Camila's family had gotten a chance to see him in action. It was up to Diego now to decide if he approved of him or not.

"My daughter is very special to me," Diego said after a minute or two had passed. "She must be cherished by her husband."

"I intend to do that."

"She deserves a home of her own. A good one—not that cabin she rents." He waved his hand in disdain. "I've seen pictures. Bah."

"I'll give her a home."

"She'll need to fly here to visit us often. Her mother misses her."

"That can be arranged. I value family, too."

"Do you?"

Carl nodded. "Unfortunately, I don't have much of it." He related the circumstances of his parents' deaths. "I'm looking forward to having a new family."

"And children?"

"I'd like that. If Camila does."

Diego surveyed him. Nodded, finally. "You have my blessing."

His pronouncement meant more to Carl than he'd anticipated, and he had to clear his throat before he could answer. "Thank you."

"Thank you," Diego said. "For helping my family find its way back together." He shook Carl's hand formally, stood up and fetched a second cup of coffee before returning to the living room.

A moment later Camila crept into the kitchen.

"Did you hear that?" Carl asked, guessing the source of the happiness shining in her eyes.

"I did. He said yes, and we didn't even have to steal the mask."

Carl stood up to cross the kitchen. "I've got to leave tonight," he said reluctantly. "I've booked a late flight. Do you think I'll be able to get a ride to Taxco?"

"Yes. I figured as much. Luis is ready when you are."

"Will you stay long?"

"No. I've already been gone for too many days. I promised Fila I'd be back. I'm planning to fly out tomorrow. Juana says she wants to come, too."

"When I'm done with Sven and Virginia, you and I need to spend some time together—alone." He cupped her face with his hands. "Have a real date, if you know what I mean."

"I think I know what you mean."

As he leaned down to kiss her, he caught himself

looking to the doorway to see if someone would arrive to stop them.

Camila did, too, then laughed.

"God, I want you," Carl groaned, pulling her into a hug instead. If he kissed her now, he didn't think he'd be able to stop, and he didn't want to appall her family just when he'd convinced them he was worthy of their daughter.

"I know," she said. "Soon."

Saying goodbye to the others was more difficult than he'd imagined. As ready as Carl was to go home, he was leaving behind some new friends here in Guerrero.

When it was time to go, Diego and Gerardo shook his hand. Arturo did, too. "We are looking forward to seeing Montana someday," he said.

Carl grinned, but worry dogged him. He had to get things right these next few days. Sven was counting on him. So was Virginia. Camila, too—and Juana— although he'd make sure they had a place to live, even if it wasn't the ranch Virginia had promised him. Still, he'd be disappointed not to follow through on his promise to Camila—and her father—sooner rather than later.

"Ready?" Camila asked him as Luis carried his bag out to his waiting truck.

"I guess so. I'll always remember this, though."

Ximena hugged Carl, too. "Make an honest woman of Camila," she scolded him. "Soon."

"Aunt Ximena!"

"I will." He turned to Paula. "Thank you for sending us here. My life is richer for having met your family."

"You are a good man," Paula told him. "I will see you soon."

"You bet." Carl pulled Camila into another fierce hug. "I'll see you back in Chance Creek."

"Can't wait," she said.

"CAMILA? WHERE HAVE you been?" Fila exclaimed when Camila called her from the airport the following day. Camila knew her roaming charges for the cross-border call would be horrible, but she needed to talk to Fila rather than text her. "Where are you? Still in Mexico? Please tell me you're coming back soon!"

"I'm sorry I haven't been in touch. It's been crazy. I can't believe how much I'll have to catch you up on. Everything okay at the restaurant?"

"Yes, but I need you back."

"I'm on my way. Waiting for my first flight. But I need to ask you something." What if she'd made Juana a promise she couldn't keep?

"Ask me what? What's going on? You're scaring me."

"My cousin. She's a really good cook. And she was wondering... well, I was wondering... if she could come to work for us. First as a volunteer," she said in a rush. "But then, if we like her, we'll need to sponsor her as a worker. She knows all about authentic Mexican cooking, something I want to learn more about. She really wants to come to Montana—"

"Of course—as long as you're coming home! We've

got plenty of work for another person. Just get on that plane, okay?" A teasing note came into her voice. "I'm sure Carl's starting to miss you."

Camila bit her lip. "Funny story about that..."

"YOU'RE DEFINITELY ON the plane tonight, right?" Sven asked when Carl took his call first thing that morning. He was just pulling into Thorn Hill after flying overnight, and there was Virginia on the front steps looking like she wanted to murder him. He'd texted her he'd be home this morning and that he'd call when he got in. Seems she hadn't wanted to wait that long.

"That's right. Any sign of the offer?" Carl parked the truck and shut off the engine.

"Not yet. But any minute, right?"

"I'd expect so."

"Well, you decided to show up," Virginia called from the front stoop. "I suppose I should be grateful."

"Who's that?" Sven asked.

"My next meeting. Gotta run. See you tonight, but let me know if you get that offer." He cut the call, gathered up the things he'd need for his talk with Virginia and climbed out of the truck, wishing he could have stopped at his cabin first to clean up.

"You're late," Virginia announced when he reached the top of the stairs. Carl passed by her into the house and kept going until he reached the formal dining room. He took a seat and set his laptop on the table.

"I'm here now. Where should we start?"

"You tell me. Tonight's the presentation to the

board—and I don't have a speech. Where is it?"

Carl straightened. "Tonight? What do you mean it's tonight? I thought we had four more days."

"It got moved. I was calling all yesterday."

He'd seen those calls. And ignored them. He'd spent hours after the party getting to the airport, then had flown all night to reach Chance Creek. He'd figured sleep was more important than soothing Virginia's nerves all over again.

Now he'd pay for that mistake.

"But—" Hell, could he fix this? Carl tapped a finger on the table. He didn't technically have to be in California until tomorrow morning. He hated to jerk Sven around more than he already had, but he could leave after the meeting tonight and arrive before the workday started.

"We'd better get right to work, then," he said resignedly. "Give me what your architect has done for you, and I'll incorporate it into the presentation. Then I'll call Sven and change my flights."

"Where's your printer?" she demanded.

"Why do I need a printer?"

"To make me a copy of my speech. What do you think I'm going to do, read that thing's mind?"

He was fast losing patience. "I'm creating a multimedia presentation, Virginia. I can't just print it out."

"I don't want a multimedia thingamajingy. I want a speech!"

Carl stopped himself from saying something he'd later regret. *She has a line on a ranch*, he reminded himself.

And I need a ranch.

"The whole point is that we're going to upgrade the school with technology to prepare Chance Creek High's students for the future. You can't convince anyone of that unless you're using technology."

She eyed his laptop askance.

Carl sighed. "I've seen your cell phone. You've sent me emails. I know you're capable of using a computer."

She shook her head. "Not like that. Not a bunch of clicking and pointing and whatever." She lifted her chin. "You'll have to come up onstage with me and run that part."

"Fine." Carl tapped on the laptop's keys, pretending to mess with the presentation while he rescheduled his flight. There was a flight out around midnight, and he'd land in San Francisco before dawn. He'd sleep on the plane. It was as simple as that.

"Pull up that presentation and let's see what you've got."

"Yes, ma'am," Carl said, wishing all of this was over. He was juggling too many balls. The search for the ranch, wooing Camila, the travel, Sven's buyout, the school update project…

One thing at a time, he told himself. *Make a list, cross things off. Get it done.* When the board had approved of the project and Sven's buyout was completed, he'd be able to concentrate on Camila and Camila alone.

He couldn't wait.

BY THE TIME she'd explained everything to Fila, it was

time to board their flight. Camila hung up, and she and Juana joined the line of passengers showing their identification and tickets before getting on the plane.

"Ready?" Camila asked her cousin.

"I think so."

It had been a teary goodbye between Juana and Camila and their respective parents. Camila had learned so much about her family in such a short period of time. "I already want to go back to visit again."

"You will," Juana assured her. "I think we'll both be traveling more now."

Camila liked the idea of that. Maybe next time her other siblings would make it to Mexico, too, and they could have a real family reunion.

The thought of it buoyed her spirits during the rest of their journey home, but by the time their third flight began its descent into the airport, she was exhausted, and Juana looked done in, too. Camila had only been in Mexico for a week, but she felt as if she had been gone for years. The relatively tame landscape was something of a relief. Not that she hadn't appreciated the colors, noise and chaos of Mexico, but she had to admit it got a little overwhelming.

Juana had kept up a cheerful running commentary throughout their flight, but toward the end she grew quiet, too. At first Camila thought she was tired, but as they waited for their turn to deplane she started to suspect it was something else. Juana clutched her carry-on so tightly her knuckles were white, and she scanned the airport through the plane windows like she was entering enemy territory.

Was she getting cold feet about coming to Montana?

Camila put a hand on her cousin's arm, determined to do whatever she could to make Juana feel at home here.

Juana had come as a tourist, and they'd agreed she'd help out at the restaurant for free while they consulted with an immigration lawyer about the correct way for Camila to sponsor her. More than likely, she'd have to go home again before coming back with a work visa. It would all take time, and Camila had assured her she could head home whenever she was ready to visit her family.

Still, she knew how intimidating it could be to enter another country. "Fila's meeting us to drive us home," she assured Juana. "Wait until you see how small the airport is. You'll think it's funny." She thought of something else. "Juana, can you keep a secret?"

"*Sí*. Of course I can."

"Good, because you can't tell anyone except Fila that I'm dating Carl."

"Why not?" Juana was taken aback.

"It's a long story. The families we live with—the Turners and the Coopers—don't like each other much. So when we see him again, pretend you're just meeting him."

"You gringos are strange."

Finally it was their turn to walk down the portable steps and cross the tarmac.

"Welcome home!" Fila cried as soon as they walked through the door into the airport. She wrapped Camila in a big bear hug. Fila's husband, Ned, was close behind her, carrying Holton, followed by all the Turners. The crowd of friendly faces chased away all her regrets about leaving Mexico.

Juana stood awkwardly to one side, watching Camila's friends cluster around her, and Camila remembered how she had felt getting off the bus in Taxco, where everybody knew everyone else, but no one knew her. She extricated herself from another of Fila's embraces and pulled Juana into the knot of greeters. "Everyone, I'd like you to meet my cousin Juana Sofia Valentin Torres."

Juana greeted the crowd timidly, and Fila embraced her the same way she had Camila. "Fila Matheson," she introduced herself. "I've heard all about you! Camila says you're going to show us how to cook real Mexican food."

Camila introduced Juana to the rest of her friends in turn, and by the end of it she thought her cousin was looking a little more like herself. Everyone else headed out when she went to collect their luggage, but Fila and Ned hung back to drive them home.

"The Turners are up in arms about this Founder's Prize," Fila warned her. "It's a good thing Carl didn't fly back with you."

Camila nodded. "I know. We'll be sneaking around for now." Something had occurred to her on the plane, and she thought maybe this was a good time to bring it up. "I should have asked this sooner," she said, "but if you're letting me and Juana make changes to the menu, it's only fair you get to do the same. Have you ever thought about offering more traditional Afghan food?"

Fila shrugged. "Not really. I love it, but all my fondest memories are of food with an American touch. The dishes my parents made. The only time I ever ate genuine Afghan food was when I was captured by the Taliban."

"That makes sense." Camila could understand why Fila didn't want to revisit that time. She'd spent ten years in Afghanistan before escaping and making her way back to the United States. For the first time Camila wondered how Juana's cooking would fit in with their fusion food.

They'd figure it out, she decided. She wouldn't worry about it now.

Fila and Juana chatted cheerfully on the ride out to the Flying W, and Maya Turner invited them in for tea when they reached the ranch.

But later, when Fila had gone, and she and Juana stepped inside her rented cabin, its musty smell assaulted her nostrils, and she hurried to throw open the living room windows, realizing she should have asked Maya or Stella to do that before she got home.

"Come on in," she told Juana, who lingered in the door. "Sorry for the mess. I left quickly. I should have cleaned up more."

Juana nodded. She stepped inside and looked around, as if afraid to venture any farther.

Camila could understand why. She'd left dishes in the sink. Something in the refrigerator smelled off, and a banana she'd left in a basket on the counter was rotten. But the day she'd left had been so hectic. She rushed around to gather the bad food, throw it all in the trash and take the bag out to the cans secured in a bear-proof container out back. Inside again, she opened more windows, sprayed some cleaner on the kitchen counters and gave everything a good wipe-down.

"I had no idea I'd be out of town more than a day or two," she explained to Juana, who finally came to join her in the living room.

"This is your house?" Juana asked.

"I'm renting it from the Turners. For now."

"I guess I thought…"

"What? That I'd live in a castle?" Camila smiled, but she wished Juana could see the charm of her little cabin. She'd never minded it until now.

"Carl will buy you a castle," Juana pronounced.

"We're going to live on a ranch when we're married. Like the one you grew up on." Hilltop Acres wasn't any fancier than her aunt and uncle's house in Mexico.

Juana didn't look like she believed her.

Camila picked up her suitcase and lugged it into her bedroom, coming back out with clean linens to make up the sofa bed for Juana. Juana watched as she pulled out the hidden bed and put on the sheets. For the first time Camila wondered what it would be like to live at Hilltop Acres. Neither she nor Carl had been exactly enthusiastic about it.

Could they make it into a home together?

Camila slowed her work, suddenly overwhelmed with shame for what she'd put Carl through. What kind of a woman forced a man to buy her a house before she'd even date him?

"Is something wrong?" Juana asked.

"Yes, there is. I need to talk to Carl." But when she called him, he didn't answer. He'd said something about an appointment earlier, and she knew he had a world of work to catch up on before he hopped in a plane and flew out to California. But later she'd try again. She needed to tell him he didn't need to own a ranch in order to be with her. She could be patient until the right one came along.

She hoped she wasn't too late. Camila wasn't all that clear on the escrow process. She had no idea if Carl would be able to cancel the sale at this point. If he couldn't, she'd gladly live with him at Hilltop Acres once their relationship had progressed that far. They'd make the best of the situation, she decided. As long as they were together, she didn't mind where it was.

"There," she said to Juana. "All set for you tonight."

"Fit for a queen," Juana said wryly. "Welcome to America."

Camila laughed out loud. "Now who's acting like a princess?"

Juana laughed, too. "Maybe I should go stay with Carl."

Camila snorted. "Good luck. His cabin is even worse than mine. Come on," she added, having a sudden inspiration.

"Where?"

"To Fila's. I'm hungry. Aren't you?

"*Sí.*"

When they arrived at Fila's Familia a half hour later, Camila braced for Juana's reaction. She hoped her cousin liked her restaurant better than she liked the cabin.

Juana stared up at the sign above the door. "It's wonderful. It looks just like the photograph," she said, "but it's real." Her eyes were shining, and Camila's heart lifted.

"You like it?"

"I love it."

"Good. Come on in. Let's get something to eat!"

Inside, the restaurant was half-full. The dinner crowd was just picking up, and they were able to snag a booth and have some privacy while they ate. She led Juana to the counter.

"Everyone loves our butter chicken nachos, and the kofta burritos are good, too," she said. "But order anything you want."

"Camila!" Fila came out from the back. "I didn't expect to see you again until tomorrow. What are you doing here?"

"We're starving," Camila told her, "and I wanted to show the place to Juana."

Fila took over and gave Juana a quick tour of the kitchen and then ushered them into seats at a booth.

"I'll play waitress today," she said. "Tell me what

you want."

A lively debate followed, and Camila helped Juana pick out a meal—an Afghan tomato salad and an order of samosas.

"They remind me of *itacates*," Juana said when her samosas arrived.

"Ita-what?" Fila asked.

"They're like tacos made out of potatoes."

"How would you make that?"

As Juana elaborated, Camila relaxed. Fila and Juana were already getting along. When her phone buzzed, Camila peeked at it. It was Stella Turner.

"Did you hear about the school board meeting tonight?" Stella asked without preamble when she took the call. "It has to do with the Coopers' plan to win the award. We're all going. What about you?"

"I don't think so. I'm pretty tired."

"Virginia's got Carl Whitfield working with her, from what I've heard. I'm worried those Coopers are going to somehow win the prize."

"Carl's working with Virginia?"

"That's right."

Camila couldn't fathom that. Either Stella was wrong, or Carl had been hiding this from her. Either way, she needed to find out. "Huh. What do you think Virginia wants the board to do?"

"I'm not sure. That's why I'm going. You should come, too."

Camila nodded. "Sure. I'll come." If Carl really was working with Virginia, why hadn't he said a word to her about it in Mexico?

And what else was he hiding?

"See, we'll make a Turner out of you yet."

.

BY THE TIME Carl entered the auditorium at Chance Creek High that evening, he was so tired he was having trouble seeing straight. He was glad it would be Virginia, not him, giving the speech. They'd spent hours going over the slides, with Sven on a video feed so he could add his two cents. At first Virginia had been put off by the video chat, but she'd gotten the hang of it and soon was ordering Sven around as much as Carl.

Carl had worried Sven would be pissed, but later, when Virginia had gone, Sven told him he welcomed the distraction. "Fulsom's got to send me that offer any minute. If I wasn't doing this, I'd be pacing a hole in my office floor."

Carl had wished him luck. Now he was the one who needed it. He spotted Steel, Lance and Olivia filing in and taking seats in the audience. He followed Virginia backstage to where the superintendent of schools, the principal and several members of the teaching staff had gathered.

"We're very interested to hear what you have to propose, Virginia," the superintendent said. "I'm Chuck Millgrove," he added and stuck out a hand to shake with Carl. "Always looking for a way to better serve the needs of our students."

"Carl Whitfield." He wondered if there was a pot of coffee around.

"I'm Geraldine Hook, Chance Creek High's principal," another woman announced. Dressed in a demure suit and sensible shoes, she looked the perfect candidate for the job.

"Nice to meet you." Carl shook with her, too.

"You think this upgrade you're proposing is the answer to Chance Creek High's problems?" Geraldine asked him.

"It may not be the cure for all of them, but it can certainly help." He wasn't on his game today, and he needed to pull himself together. He couldn't assume everyone would be on their side, even if he felt they were making a worthy contribution to the school.

"Do you even know what Chance Creek High's problems are?" she challenged him.

Carl opened his mouth, but the smooth answer he could normally count on didn't jump to mind. *Did* he know what the problems were?

He realized he'd never even thought to ask. He turned to Virginia to include her in the conversation, but Millgrove announced, "Time, people."

Geraldine Hook lifted an eyebrow, as if sensing Carl's relief at the interruption, then turned away, her disdain clear.

Carl watched Millgrove help Virginia to a seat on the stage and wondered at the source of the man's almost overblown deference to her. Was there more to this school deal than he knew? Virginia liked to manipulate people. Was she manipulating Millgrove?

Not for the first time, Carl wished he'd moved faster on the Hilltop Acres. He didn't like being in Virginia's thrall. But he was proposing a plan to bring Chance Creek High into the twenty-first century. There was nothing wrong with that. In fact, if there wasn't so much riding on the outcome, he'd be energized by this situation. He loved technology, and Chance Creek was his town. He was going to marry Camila. Have kids of his own. They'd go to the high school.

Carl straightened up. He'd let himself get overpowered by the details, but the important thing was he would be making a difference to his neighbors. So what if Virginia had been the driving force? Maybe this would be the start of a new era in Chance Creek. While some ranch owners were quite prosperous, others scrambled to hold their heads above water. There weren't a lot of choices for young folks in this town, and a lot of them ended up moving somewhere else. If Chance Creek could diversify, more of them could stay. Families could stick together and help one another. That would lead to greater prosperity for all of them.

When he saw Olivia, Steel and Lance sitting by themselves over to one side in the audience, he hoped this initiative would end up helping them, too. Maybe once they'd experienced doing something good for the town, they'd feel more of a kinship with the other people who lived here. They mostly kept themselves to themselves, except for Lance, whose friends Carl didn't like. If they felt more confident of their welcome, they could branch out and meet people who were more positive in their thoughts and actions.

Carl decided he'd throw himself heart and soul into the proceedings tonight—not to get access to a ranch for himself but to help a family who'd helped him these past few years. Olivia, Lance and Steel deserved a chance.

"What are they doing here?" Virginia cut into his thoughts, pointing toward the back of the auditorium.

Carl followed her gaze and caught sight of Stella, Maya, Liam and Noah making their way down the central aisle to a row of seats near the front. His heart sank. He'd hoped the Turners would keep clear of the meeting. Were they here to cause trouble?

When Camila entered the auditorium, he stifled a groan. He should have known she'd find out about what he was doing, but he'd hoped she wouldn't until after the meeting—when the school board's decision had already been made, and Virginia had put him in touch with the owner of the ranch like she'd promised him. It wasn't that he was ashamed of helping the Coopers; he simply didn't want Camila to know that he'd lost the Hilltop Acres until he had something better to offer her.

Camila stood in the back, scanning the seated crowd, but when she lifted her gaze to him, he made a snap decision and pointed to the door behind her.

"Be right back," he told Virginia. He didn't want to worry through the presentation what Camila was thinking. He wondered why Camila had come. What had she heard? Was she here as an honorary Turner?

He slipped out the side door and paced the halls of the school until he found her. "Hey," he said.

"Hey, yourself. What's going on?"

Carl gave her the quickest rundown he could. "Virginia wants the Founder's Prize. Came up with an idea to upgrade the high school. Pitched it to me, and I got involved. I think it's a good idea." All of which was true—up to a point.

"Okay. Well, good luck, I guess." She didn't seem too impressed, and Carl knew he had to make up for keeping this from her.

"I don't think the Turners will like it much," he confessed. "Wasn't sure you'd like it, either."

Camila relented. "I'm not going to let this damn Turner/Cooper feud get between us, Carl."

"You aren't mad?"

"That you're helping to upgrade Chance Creek High? No. But I'm miffed you didn't think you could tell me."

"I was being an idiot. I don't want to lose you."

"You're not going to lose me."

"Then I won't make that mistake again."

"Good," she said with a grin.

They heard the amplified sound of someone coughing into the microphone onstage. "Testing—one, two, three."

"You'd better get back in there."

"Where's Juana?"

"Hanging out at the restaurant with Fila. She's going to help with closing tonight."

"Got it. Well, I'd better go." He hesitated, still wishing he could spill everything to Camila. Wishing he could push her against the wall and kiss her silly. There wasn't time, though. He handed her his phone. "Do me a favor? Hold this for me. I don't need any distractions tonight."

Camila looked at it skeptically. "Why not just turn it off?"

Carl was already shaking his head. "Sven's going to get his offer from Fulsom any minute. When he does, he'll call me, and I'll feel it whether or not it's turned on. Like a phantom ringtone. I just want to concentrate on one thing while I'm up there."

She chuckled. "Okay, I'll hold on to it."

"Thanks. See you when it's over." Carl raced back to the stage, where Chuck Millgrove had just walked up to the podium, greeted the audience and introduced Virginia.

"It's not every day that I have such good news to announce," he said. "But Virginia Cooper, here, has taken it upon herself to spearhead a campaign to upgrade Chance Creek High and start an exciting new program at the school. I'll let Virginia Cooper spell out the project, and afterward there will be time for questions."

Virginia stood to a smattering of applause, marred by the creaks of a lot of people shifting uncomfortably in their wooden seats. Tension tightened Carl's shoulders. He'd been so busy this afternoon, he'd forgotten how unpopular Virginia was in town. And how the Cooper family in general were viewed as troublemakers. The Turners' presence front and center in the crowd boded ill for how this presentation would go. He could only hope they listened and didn't disrupt it. He saw Camila take her seat with the others.

Virginia took her place at the podium. Carl joined her to work the laptop. "We all know Chance Creek High has always been a disappointment as a school," she began.

Instantly Liam Turner jumped to his feet. "Shut your mouth, you good-for-nothing—"

Stella pulled him down into his seat with a thump. "Hush."

"I'm not going to hush while—"

"A disappointment as a school!" Virginia repeated, moving her mouth so close to the microphone on the lectern the feedback screeched and everyone winced. "But that's all going to change," she went on, pulling back a couple of inches. "Thanks to us Coopers. We've found the money. We've found the talent. We're going to bring this town into the twenty-first century!"

Silence greeted this pronouncement. Camila's horrified expression was echoed on other people's faces throughout the auditorium.

"We're going to obliterate everything about the high school that makes it an utter failure—"

"You're the failure!" Liam called out.

A couple and their child got up and left the auditorium. Carl saw others gathering their belongings. Getting ready to leave.

He met Camila's gaze. *Do something!* she mouthed.

She was right; he had to salvage this before Virginia

ruined everything.

He did the only thing he could: grabbed the microphone from Virginia's hand and elbowed her aside. "Virginia, thank you for that interesting introduction to the project that Andersson Robotics wants to bring to Chance Creek."

He fixed Virginia with a hard stare until she backed away, pressing her lips together in a tight line, and left the stage. Carl knew there'd be hell to pay later, but he didn't care about that. He wasn't going to let Virginia deprive the town's students of a chance to improve their lot in life out of her petty need to run the Turners down.

It had been a while since he'd stood onstage to present to a large crowd, and the audience looked ready to mutiny, but Carl remembered this adrenaline rush. He'd always loved speaking to potential clients and business partners, which is part of the reason he'd done so well. Why had he been so quick to give this up? he wondered as he gathered his thoughts. This was one of his strengths. Surely there were opportunities for a rancher to work a crowd, too.

Or were there?

"When I look around Chance Creek High," he began, putting the question away for later, "I see a lot of hard work and love. I see teachers who come in here every day and give it their all. I see an administration who goes to the wall to get their staff what they need to do a good job. I see families, parents volunteering their time to help out. But I'll be frank. What I don't see is money." He let the phrase stand, its echoes rippling throughout the auditorium.

A couple of people sat down again.

"Everyone knows it's not easy to be a rancher or to live in a small town in a ranching community. There aren't a lot of jobs around. With help from the Coopers and Andersson Robotics, I want to change all that. We all love this town. We want to stay here—and we want our kids to stay here, too. So we need new businesses, new ideas and new techniques to keep our economy viable. That's what this project is all about."

He had their attention now.

"We'll start by fixing the high school's roof and bringing its wiring up to code. Then we'll make sure every classroom has the technology it needs to function at its best. Last, but certainly not least, we'll build out the Andersson Robotics wing, complete with everything your children will need to graduate ready to participate in the jobs of the future."

Carl moved on to specifics about each phase of the upgrade. When he caught Camila's eye again, she was smiling and nodding, although she glanced at the Turners clustered around her and quickly toned down her reaction. She looked down suddenly, pulled out a phone and put it to her ear. He saw her get up and leave the auditorium, but a woman had stood up to ask a question, and Carl turned his attention to her.

"Hi, I'm Deborah Axman, and I teach tenth grade English," she said. "Everything you said so far tonight has been interesting, and I know that we need more technology in the classrooms, but here's the thing: I already have my curriculum prepared for next year. If there is going to be new technology in my classroom—and a whole new program many of the kids are going to want to participate in—how will that affect what I need to prepare? I don't know how to use the technology you're talking about. How can I teach it? How much training will I get? Is my time going to be compensated?"

A chorus of cheers and assenting voices filled the air. Carl scrambled to answer.

"I… I don't entirely have an answer to that," he said truthfully. He hadn't even thought about it. Sven had promised to provide training, but Deborah was right; there wouldn't be much time.

"Are these computers and interfaces going to take up space in my room?" another teacher asked. "Are you handing out laptops or tablets to every student? Or will they have to share? Sharing can be really disruptive."

"Who's going to teach the robotics classes? How many students will be able to participate? Is the program going to be separate or integrated with other classes?" a man asked. Carl didn't know if he was a teacher or a parent.

As more people stood up to ask their questions, he realized with a sinking feeling this meeting wasn't going to be nearly enough. The school board was supposed to vote on the idea tonight, but how could they do that without all the information?

Liam Turner stood up next. "This is what you get

when a Cooper runs the show. A mess! Virginia Cooper doesn't care about robotics. All she cares is about herself!"

Lance Cooper jumped to his feet. "All you Turners care about is keeping the rest of us in the past!"

"We don't need your stupid upgrade. We'd all be better off if you just left!"

"It's you Turners who need to leave."

The two men advanced on one another, hopping over rows of seats and pushing past other audience members to get within reach.

"There's going to be a fight!" someone yelled.

Carl rubbed a hand over his face.

Of course there was.

WHEN CAMILA'S PHONE buzzed in her pocket, she pulled it out and answered it before realizing it was Carl's. "Camila here. Whoops. I mean, hi. Uh… Carl's phone."

"Dude, they sent—" The man on the other end of the line cleared his throat. "Oh, sorry. Think I got the wrong number."

"Sven?" Camila guessed. "Sven, wait." When Carl had announced Andersson Robotics was partnering with him on the technology upgrade, she'd put two and two together and realized this was part of the reason he and Sven talked all the time. She had no idea why Carl hadn't told her, even if he was helping the Coopers to the detriment of the Turners. The end result would help all of Chance Creek's students.

Up onstage, Carl was finishing his presentation, so she slipped out of her seat and quickly left the auditorium as people stood up to ask questions.

Sven hesitated. "Who is this?"

"Camila. Carl's—a good friend. I'm holding on to his phone while he gives his presentation about the robotics program. The idea sounds wonderful. You're amazing for partnering with him on this."

"Thanks."

"Is that why you're calling?

"Uh… No. How's it going, though?"

"The presentation was awesome. Now people are asking questions." She peeked inside. "Hard questions, by the sound of it."

"Huh. I thought everyone would love the idea."

"Not everyone," she said as more people stood up. Carl was fielding questions as best he could. "Want me to take a message?"

Sven sighed. "Yeah. I was hoping to talk to him, but I guess he's busy. Tell him I got Fulsom's offer, and it sucks. It's so low it's insulting. Now I've got two days to accept it, or it'll disappear."

That sounded bad. "Anything else?"

"He knows the rest. He needs to get here tonight. I need his help. I don't know what to do. Should I counter? Tell Fulsom to go to hell?" Sven's voice rose.

Camila turned at a shout from inside the auditorium. She stole a look through the door. Liam was yelling at Carl.

"What do *you* think you should do?" she asked Sven,

wanting to keep him on the line. The man sounded upset, and she knew Carl meant to fly to California tonight—but things didn't look like they were going very well at his presentation.

"What do you mean?" Sven asked.

"What does your gut say?" Carl was always talking about his gut—how it told him what to do when he had hard decisions to make.

There was silence for a moment. "My gut says turn it down. I think they're lowballing me because they know I'm new at this and they want to see if I'll flinch. If I decline, they'll realize I'm not playing around. Then maybe they'll make a serious offer."

"That sounds smart to me." Now Lance Cooper was yelling at Liam. They were both standing. Advancing on each other.

"But what if I'm wrong?" Sven persisted. "I owe it to my company, my employees, to be a hundred percent sure what the right call is."

"Is that even possible?" Camila asked as Liam and Lance faced off with each other. "What would happen if the deal falls through? Would you go belly up?"

"No. My company is a money-making machine! Lots of other companies will want to buy it—"

"Then why are you so scared to take a chance?"

"I don't know." Sven was silent for a long time. "You're right. I don't know why I'm scared. Hell, Fulsom's the one who should be scared—maybe I'll sell Andersson Robotics to someone else. Or maybe I'll keep it."

"There you go—that's more like it," Camila encouraged him, but her heart was in her mouth. Liam and Lance were nearly nose to nose, yelling and threatening each other. The other Turners and Coopers had gathered around. "Sven—I've got a problem here." She looked at Carl onstage, speaking loudly into the microphone, trying to get people's attention.

"What's wrong?"

"It's the presentation. It's about to become a riot."

"What happened?"

"The teachers were upset about how they'd get trained in time for the fall, and then—" she didn't know how to explain the Coopers and Turners "—tensions flared," she said. An understatement, if she'd ever made one.

"What's Carl doing?"

"Trying to reason with them. It's not working."

"Get me to him. Can you do that? Safely?" All Sven's indecision was gone.

"Yes." She was in no danger on this side of the auditorium, and if Sven thought he could help Carl, she'd do what it took to get him up to the stage. She slipped back inside and ran along the edge of the large room to the stage. "Carl!"

He didn't hear her until she'd raced up the stage and crossed to him. "Carl—it's Sven!"

"I can't talk now. I've got a bit of a situation here," he said.

Camila would have laughed if it wasn't so awful. "Sven's got an idea!"

Carl took his phone just as Liam swung the first punch down in the audience. Lance threw one back. Carl listened a moment, said something, listened again and then nodded. He put two fingers in his mouth, leaned down close to the microphone and whistled. The shrieking sound and feedback made everyone in the auditorium duck.

"Everyone in their seats. NOW!" Carl roared.

Camila clapped a hand to her mouth and nearly sat down on the stage. In the audience, people took their seats quickly. Even Liam and Lance backed away from each other.

"You wanted answers—I've got answers. I've got the head of Andersson Robotics on the line, and he'd like to tell you exactly how he plans to phase in the robotics program in a sensible way over the next two years. He'd also like to explain how the infrastructure will be laid over the summer months so that there won't be any interference in the fall, and how every teacher will receive paid training so that they can integrate the new technology in a way that won't put an undue burden on them now." He fiddled with his laptop, and a man's face filled the screen behind Carl.

"Hi, I'm Sven Andersson," the man said. "Let me tell you about Andersson Robotics."

Camila listened along with everyone else to Sven's description of the way he meant to bring their school into the future. She was so glad she'd taken Sven's call. So glad he and Carl had turned this around. They would do good work here—with or without the Coopers and the Turners.

"THE VOTE IS unanimous," Millgrove said when the meeting drew to a close. "We have approved the Cooper Andersson Robotics project."

Carl breathed a sigh of relief, even though it had been obvious by the end of Sven's presentation that the majority of teachers and parents in the audience supported the project. He didn't know what he would have done if it had been turned down—or if Sven hadn't called.

"Guess I'd better get to the airport," Carl told Sven as everyone stood up around him. He shifted their connection back to a private call. "That was good work. You're a quick thinker." He couldn't believe the way Sven had managed to answer everyone's questions.

"We've done so much training over the years, it wasn't hard to extrapolate out what we'd need to do in Chance Creek. Besides, I was a TA back in college, remember? I've had to write curriculum myself. I know what these teachers are up against."

"I didn't know that."

"This project of yours is right up my alley, actually. If I wasn't so swamped, I'd probably be there right now immersed in the whole thing."

"Speaking of which, what's going on with Fulsom?"

Sven laughed. "He sent me the offer. Totally low-balled me. I'm going to turn him down."

"What?"

"It was Camila's idea."

"Wait… Camila told you to turn Fulsom down?"

"Not exactly. She told me to trust my gut. I called in a panic about it and wanted to talk to you. She settled me down, said you were busy, then talked me through it. I realized she was right; I'm not going to let Fulsom push me around. Andersson Robotics is a great company. And Fulsom isn't the only game in town."

Carl couldn't think when he heard Sven sound so confident. "That sounds like a smart way to look at it. When I land, we can think of a counteroffer if you like."

"Carl, you don't have to fly out here," Sven said. "I appreciate everything you've done for me all along, and anytime you want to come hang out, I'll be glad to see you. But you've got so much going on there, and I think it's time for me to start answering my own questions."

"I don't mind," Carl told him.

"I know. Thanks for that. But you've got a ranch to buy, don't you?"

"I hope so."

"Go get it done. And say thanks again to Camila. She said the right thing at the right time. Hope I get to meet her soon."

"I hope so, too." Carl spotted Camila waiting for him. "Gotta go. You sure you don't need me to come out there?"

"I'm sure. I'll call you tomorrow and let you know what happens. I think I'm going to let Fulsom stew tonight."

"I like it. Good luck."

"Right back at you."

Sven cut the call, and Carl went to Camila. "Ready to get out of here?"

"Heck, yeah. That was intense."

"You're telling me."

He caught sight of Virginia deep in conversation with Millgrove and decided it was the perfect time to slip out. "Let's go before anyone sees us."

"Sounds good to me."

Outside the night was still warm. "Don't you need to go to California?" Camila asked when they reached Carl's truck.

"Sven doesn't need me, after all. Because a certain smart chef walked him through his problem."

"Really?" Camila bit her lip. "I hope I said the right thing."

"I think you did." He maneuvered her up against the truck. "I miss you. I swear to God I'm not going to let another moment pass before I do this." He bent down, gathered Camila into his arms—and kissed her.

CAMILA KNEW SHE should get back to Juana. She'd ridden to the meeting with Stella and Maya, and Juana had stayed with Fila at the restaurant. They'd been chatting happily the last time she saw them, but it was late now. Soon Fila would be closing up shop.

She couldn't seem to stop kissing Carl, though. If they weren't standing in the high school parking lot, she'd be doing a lot more.

She'd dreamed for years about touching Carl like this. Now his hands were gripping her hips, her breasts were pressed against his chest and his mouth moved over hers like he was ravenous. She'd tangled her fingers in his hair, gone up on tiptoe and was holding on for dear life. This was what she'd been waiting for—and she never wanted to stop now that they'd started.

When they finally broke apart, she could see Carl fight for control. "Can I give you a ride home?" he asked, his voice husky.

"To the restaurant," she said. "Or I can walk. It's only a few blocks."

"Let's ride."

"Okay," she answered readily. She wanted all the time with him she could get. She didn't want to stop touching him, and he seemed to feel the same way, but they separated and climbed into his truck.

"I can't believe this school thing is over," he said when they were on the road.

"Hardly. Now the board has approved the project, I'd say your work is just beginning."

"Sven will help."

She didn't know how she was managing to keep talking after that kiss. Her hands were shaking. "He seems like a good guy."

"He is."

"You are, too, for caring so much about the kids in this town." She touched his arm and wished she was sitting closer to him. This was a big truck, and there was a lot of room between them. But just as she was considering how to slide closer, Carl sighed.

"I've got a confession to make."

She wasn't sure she liked the sound of that. "What?"

"I didn't do it for the kids. Not at first, anyway. Virginia strong-armed me into it."

Camila chuckled. "I guess I shouldn't be surprised. She's... well, she's Virginia. How did she manage it?"

"That's the bad part." Carl concentrated on the road. "We lost Hilltop Acres."

Camila wasn't prepared for that, and she gripped the armrest, trying to swallow her disappointment. "Lost it? How?"

"Before I ever managed to put a bid on it, someone else snatched it up, and the owner didn't even give me a chance to counteroffer. Virginia was behind it. Somehow."

"So why did you help her?" Camila couldn't believe it. Now they didn't have a ranch? They were starting all over again.

"Because she said she had a line on a better one, and if I helped her get the project approved, she'd make sure I had a chance at it. Camila, I don't deserve your trust after keeping this back from you, but will you give me a little more time? As annoying as Virginia is, I don't think she's lying. But I won't know until I see the property she has in mind."

"This is my fault," Camila said, sinking down in her seat. "This whole thing. I should have said right from the start I needed to take it slow. I shouldn't have made it about you owning a ranch or not owning one. You never would have had to go through this."

"I'm kind of glad I went through it, though," Carl

admitted. "Not waiting three years to kiss you—but the rest of this. Working with Sven. Upgrading the school. I want to be involved in this town, and this project makes feel like I really am. And now I want a ranch," he added. "Virginia better not let me down."

"I hope she doesn't, but whatever happens, I'm ready to be with you," Camila blurted. "I'm done waiting for things to be perfect. I want to start living."

"You mean that?" Carl turned to her.

"Definitely."

He put on his signal and turned onto the highway out of town.

"Where are we going?" Camila squeaked, holding on to the armrest as he took the corner fast.

"Somewhere private."

His jaw was set, his focus on the road ahead of him. He drove a few miles, passed the Flying W, kept going, and finally pulled off the road down a lane and parked.

"Where are we?"

"Settler's Ridge."

"The ranch the Coopers and Turners are fighting over?"

"That's right. Tonight it's ours. Come over here." He held out a hand.

Heat flared inside Camila. Hell, yeah. This was exactly what she wanted. It had been torture being so close to him in Mexico and hardly getting to touch him. She'd been buzzing ever since the day he'd told her he'd found a ranch. Wanting him so badly she could hardly think of anything else. After their kiss earlier, she'd known she wouldn't sleep tonight.

Why shouldn't they take this chance? This past week all they'd done was what other people wanted them to. Now it was their turn. She undid her belt and clambered as gracefully as she could to where he was sitting. He lifted her onto his lap, and she straddled him, her skirt hiking up high on her thighs. His desire for her was immediately clear, and her hunger for him flared hot. Camila wriggled a little against him, and he groaned.

"That's better."

The desire in his voice kicked her pulse up higher, and when he kissed her, Camila melted against him. This was exactly where she wanted to be. Her hands braced on Carl's strong chest, his hands on her hips, moving her against his hardness.

A fire of need kindled hot inside her, and soon Camila wanted much more. When Carl reached between them to undo the buttons of her blouse, she found the hem of his shirt and urged it up over his head. Carl finished with her buttons, and she wriggled out of her sleeves, her shirt soon meeting his on the passenger seat.

Carl ran a finger along the lace edge of her bra, and Camila's breath caught. When he reached around to unclasp it, she gladly let him take it off. It joined the growing pile of their clothes, and Camila moaned as Carl palmed her breasts. God, that felt good.

This was the perfect position to allow him access to them. Her nipples were already hard, and each stroke of his hand over her sensitive skin brought another wave of desire through her. When he bent to take one nipple into his mouth, Camila closed her eyes and arched her back. His touch was wonderful, and she wanted to feel his hands everywhere on her body.

He took his time exploring her. Teasing her nipples. Laving them with his tongue.

Camila wasn't wearing stockings, so when Carl reached under her skirt and stroked his hands up her thighs, a shot of heat went straight to her core. He tugged at the band of her thong, and she maneuvered her way out of it—not an easy feat. By the time she was done, they were laughing. Camila wrestled with the belt and button of Carl's jeans. He was so hard when she got him free, she was in no doubt of how he felt about her.

"I want to be in you." Carl's ragged voice undid her.

"I want that, too."

"Oh, yeah?"

Camila nodded.

"Protection?"

"I'm on the Pill. Carl, please—"

He must have understood what she needed. He lifted her, shifted into place, then lowered her down and pushed inside, filling her in the most exquisite way. When he began to move, it took everything she had not to come right then. He was so hard. So incredible.

But she wanted this encounter to last.

Her hands on Carl's shoulders, her hips moving up and down, she met his gaze and tried to show him everything she was feeling. This was all she'd ever wanted. All she'd dreamed about these past few years.

And here they were.

Together.

As she rocked against him, her nipples brushed his chest, sending tingles of pleasure throughout her body. His muscles rippled as he gripped her hips, guiding her movements, speeding her up. She clung to him as Carl increased his pace, until all she could do was arch her back and hold on for the ride.

She'd waited so long for this, she couldn't hold back anymore. Camila cried out as Carl's thrusts sped up, the delicious friction sending her over the edge. Carl bucked with his release and set Camila off on another orgasm. By the time it was over, she could hardly breathe and collapsed against him, laughing—

Almost in tears.

"You okay?" Carl gasped, fighting to recover his breath, too.

"Yes." She'd never felt like this—never had her body thrum with joy after making love to a man. This wasn't ordinary. This could only happen with Carl. "We work together."

"Hell, yeah, we do." Carl chuckled. He ran his hands up to cup her breasts again. "We certainly do."

Chapter Eight

"FULSOM COUNTERED MY counteroffer, and I took it. The deal's done," Sven shouted when Carl answered his phone the following morning as he stepped out of the shower. "I got everything I wanted and more!"

"Congratulations," Carl told him, grabbing a towel and wrapping it around his waist. He headed into his bedroom and dried off while Sven told him all about it. "Sounds like you handled it perfectly."

"Thanks to Camila. Don't let her go, man. That woman's one in a million."

"I plan to keep her around as long as she'll let me," Carl said, pulling clothes out of his closet. He tossed the towel aside and tugged on a pair of boxer briefs. He'd had to take her to the restaurant last night, and it had been hell to let her out of his sight, but they'd be together again soon. "Did you sign the paperwork with Fulsom already?"

"My lawyers are going over it, but so far, so good. This is really happening," Sven added. "I'm shaking, man. I can't believe it."

"It's exciting, isn't it?" Carl grabbed his jeans. Pulled

them on.

"Yeah." He paused. "Hey, I've got another call. I gotta go, but I wanted to thank you for everything you've done for me. I know I've been a bit of a pest."

"Not at all. You helped me, too."

"Looking forward to doing a lot more of that just as soon as this deal is in the bag. I added language to the contract so Fulsom can't back out of supporting the school upgrade even when he takes over my company, by the way. When I can, I plan to come out and lend a hand."

"Looking forward to it."

They said their goodbyes and hung up. Carl had just finished dressing when someone pounded on his front door. He crossed through the cabin to open it and found Virginia on the front stoop, her umbrella in her hand.

"I don't know whether to shake your hand or bash your head in," she announced, stepping over the threshold.

"The board approved the project," Carl reminded her.

"No thanks to you. You nearly blew it. Your friend had to save the day. I should be showing *him* a ranch."

Carl bit back the first answer that sprang to his lips. "Is that why you're here? To show me a ranch?" he asked.

"I'm not here to socialize."

"Looks like you've got the Founder's Prize in the palm of your hand."

"That's right. Come fall, Settler's Ridge will be Cooper land."

Carl didn't remind her that the Turners—and everyone else—still had months to try to even the score. No need to rile Virginia.

Twenty minutes later she directed him to drive up toward a wrought-iron gate that blocked the entry to a ranch Carl had heard about but never visited.

"Laurel Heights is a jewel," Virginia told him. "Nothing can rival Thorn Hill, of course, but Laurel Heights comes close. Fifteen hundred acres. All usable land, except the high ground in the northeast corner. Only a little farther out from town than Thorn Hill. Handy for a city slicker like you."

She would have made a good real estate agent, Carl thought as the gate opened automatically. Better than Megan Lawrence, who'd never managed to find him a property like this. As they drove up the winding paved road, Carl had a feeling this ranch outstripped Thorn Hill in every way imaginable. He could tell it had achieved a prosperity Virginia's property never had, but he knew she valued Thorn Hill for its history more than anything else.

Carl was grateful for that; he didn't want to compete with anyone else for Laurel Heights, judging by the look of the place so far. After several minutes, the carefully trimmed shrubbery that lined both sides of the drive fell away, and the vista that appeared brought Carl's heart into his throat. An almost palatial home sat atop a rise of ground, looking out over a spread of pastures, brush and forest in the distance. "It's—" He broke off and cleared his throat, suddenly struggling to speak. "It's beautiful." He slowed the car to a stop and sat looking at it all. "Don't pull my leg on this one. I couldn't stand it," he said truthfully.

"I'm not pulling your leg. You did something for my family, and I reward that kind of loyalty," Virginia said complacently.

Loyalty. Carl swallowed. Would she feel the same way if she knew about his relationship with Camila? She'd better not find out until the deed was in his hands.

"I'll want a fast sale," he said. "I don't want to be screwed around again."

"The seller is aware of that. It works in his favor, too. He needs to be in Dubai by the end of the week."

"Dubai?" He decided he'd better not ask, although he was certainly curious.

"Oil business," Virginia said succinctly. "This is a trophy ranch. A prosperous ranch, nonetheless, but it's a trophy, not a real home. You'll have to fix that, I suppose."

When they met the owner and toured the main house, Carl began to understand what Virginia meant. Everything was perfect, but nothing was homely about the residence. He wondered what Camila would make of it. At least there would be plenty of room for her family to stay when they visited.

An hour later their tour was done, and the owner, Charles Cassidy, and his agent, Mark Fontaine, had appeared with paperwork. Virginia wandered off, bored with the proceedings, and poked around a formal rose garden. The deal didn't take long to hammer out. Carl was offering cash and the full price. He'd known the minute he'd seen the property it was the right one.

"Do you have a date in mind for closing?" Mark Fontaine asked.

"A week from today?" Carl ventured. He had a feeling Cassidy wouldn't balk, and he was right.

"A week it is," Fontaine said after a nod from Cassidy.

"A pleasure doing business with you, Mr. Whitfield." Cassidy shook Carl's hand.

"I'm looking to keep this quiet for now," Carl told him. "That all right with you?"

"Fine with me. I'm not in town much, anyway."

"Good luck in Dubai."

"Enjoy your new ranch."

Carl still couldn't believe the man could walk away from a place like this. A few minutes later it was all over, and Cassidy and Fontaine had gone, telling him to stay and explore the property as long as he wanted to.

"All settled?" Virginia asked, joining Carl at his truck.

"All settled."

"You'll be moving soon, then?"

"Yep." He wouldn't tell her how soon. "Keep it to yourself, though. I don't want to jinx it. And if this deal falls through for any reason, I'll make sure Sven reneges on his promise about the school. Got it?"

"Whatever," Virginia said, but he was sure he'd just

bought her silence. He opened the door for her, and she settled herself in the passenger seat.

"Speaking of which," Carl went on. "It was mighty convenient for you that the owner of Hilltop Acres decided to sell to someone else right when you needed me to help with the school." That had bothered him for a while.

Virginia shrugged. "A very deserving couple bought it. The wife is the granddaughter of someone I know at the Prairie Garden. What would have been a small property for you was the perfect size for them. Funny how these things go."

"Yeah, funny." Meddlesome woman had nearly messed up everything for him.

"Funny how losing Hilltop Acres ended with you finding the ranch of your dreams," she added tartly.

Carl couldn't help but chuckle as he shut her door and walked around the truck.

Hell. She was right.

"WE'RE BACK," FILA said when she and Juana burst into the restaurant laden with shopping bags. While they'd prepped the food earlier that morning, Fila had pushed Juana to think of a special dish to cook up for the lunch crowd and then had taken Juana to the grocery store to buy the ingredients.

Camila was thankful to her friend for helping Juana like that. While her cousin's initial trepidation seemed to have calmed down, she still seemed overwhelmed at times. Camila wanted to make the transition easy, but she was still finding it hard to think of anything except being with Carl the other night.

She couldn't wait until they were alone again, but she wasn't sure when that would be. All Carl had said when he dropped her at the restaurant that night was he'd call... soon.

"Did you find everything you needed?" She caught sight of Juana's face and paused. Juana didn't look happy.

"We did our best," Fila said.

"Everything is so different here," Juana exclaimed. "None of the fruits and vegetables are fresh enough, the masa flour is too processed, the cheeses and spices are all wrong."

Camila glanced at Fila, and Fila shrugged. "My mom taught me to cook an Americanized version of our culture's food, so she was the one who had to struggle with the differences, not me."

Juana hastened to say, "I mean no criticism, but tiny differences add up." She pulled a tomato out of a bag, lifted it to her nose and sniffed it. "This is red, but it doesn't smell ripe. No wonder you put sugar in your salsa."

Camila nodded. Her father had complained about the same things all her life. "What did you decide to make?"

"Chiles en nogada." She saw Camila's confusion and explained, "It's a lot like *chiles rellenos* but served on celebratory occasions. The dish incorporates the colors of our flag: green chile peppers, a creamy white nut

sauce and sweet red pomegranate seeds."

"That sounds—" Camila paused. It sounded far too strange to catch on in Chance Creek. Hot peppers and cream? Pomegranate seeds? That was a stretch. But Juana was grinning ear to ear, and she had to admit a dish that physically embodied the Mexican flag seemed like a fitting way to introduce their new authentic Mexican recipes.

"That sounds perfect," she made herself say.

Juana set to work while Camila and Fila went about their usual chores getting ready for the lunch crowd. They'd decided to offer samples of Juana's dish to everyone—and see how many people ordered it. Fila made a big sign to advertise the special entrée and posted it near the cash register. Bess, who ran the till, also handed out the samples.

As people began to trickle in, Juana hovered over the stove, making sure to be ready to dish out plates, but as the minutes ticked by, no orders came for the *chiles en nogada,* and Camila began to wish Fila had pressed Juana to make a simpler dish.

"Don't worry," she told her cousin. "The lunch crush has just started. Things will pick up."

Things did pick up—for her and Fila. Finally someone ordered Juana's dish, and Juana jumped into action, quickly serving it up and passing it through the window to the front of the restaurant. But then more minutes ticked by and no more orders came.

Camila was as hard-pressed as usual to keep up with preparing their stock dishes, but when she looked up and caught Juana blinking rapidly, her chin lifted in the air in a valiant attempt to hold back tears, she knew she had to do something.

"Be back in a minute." She ducked into the restroom, pulled out her phone and called Mia Matheson, Fila's sister-in-law. "Mia? Have you had lunch yet?" She explained the situation as quickly as possible. "Can you grab a few people and come order Juana's dish? It's killing me to watch her, and really the dish is great if you know what to expect." She'd sampled it earlier and realized her mother had served it sometimes when they were kids. She simply hadn't thought of it in years.

"I'm on it," Mia said.

Twenty minutes later several orders for Juana's dish rolled in. And then a few more. And then a few more. Camila said a silent thank-you to Mia for obviously rounding up a bunch of their friends. Juana was beaming now, especially when Bess called in through the window, "The Mathesons want to meet the new chef!"

"Come on," Camila told Juana. "Let's go show you off." She led Juana out to the main part of the restaurant and made the introductions. "Juana, this is Mia Matheson, her husband, Luke, his brother, Jake, and his wife, Hannah, and Fila's mother-in-law, Lisa."

"Your cooking is divine," Lisa said. "I've never tasted anything like it. Pomegranate seeds in a nut sauce. What will they think of next?"

"Thank you," Juana said shyly. "It is a very traditional meal in my country."

"I can see why. It's yummy," Hannah said. "Totally

different from anything I've ever had."

"I had to make Luke try it," Mia confided, "but even he thinks it's good."

"I'm more of a hamburger kind of guy," Luke said. "I didn't think I'd like this, but I do."

Juana took that in. "Maybe it's too… strange… to start with? Should I try something more familiar?" she asked.

Camila held her breath; she hadn't wanted to dictate that course of action to Juana, but now her cousin was making the connection herself.

Luke nodded. "Around here folks are kind of traditional. Some people are adventurous when it comes to food, but a lot of us aren't. We like beef. Do you know how to make anything with beef?"

"Sí!" Juana nodded her head.

"Something that looks kind of like something I might have eaten before?"

She thought about this.

"What if you took a traditional Mexican beef dish of some kind and wrapped it in a tortilla?" Hannah suggested. "We eat burritos all the time."

"Burritos?" Juana sighed and nodded. Camila knew why: Mexicans didn't eat them the way Americans did. *"Sí.* I can make delicious burritos."

"But not too spicy," Mia cautioned.

"Not too spicy," Luke confirmed. "A man likes to be able to taste his food."

"Not too spicy," Juana agreed. "I can do that. I guess." She made a face.

Camila laughed along with the rest of the group. "We'd better get back to the kitchen." As she ushered a much happier Juana back to the swinging doors, a new group of customers walked into the restaurant.

"Ooh, what's that?" Camila heard a woman ask.

"It's new," Mia told her. "You can try a sample at the counter. It's amazing."

"CAN YOU COME for a ride? I need to show you something," Carl asked several days later when he arrived at Fila's Familia just after nine.

Camila glanced back at the kitchen to find Fila waving her away. "We've got this," she called out. Juana was helping her prep food. She'd come a long way during the week and already moved around the restaurant kitchen like she'd been working there for years. Over the past couple of days, she'd designed several different burrito fillings and kept offering taste tests to the customers, keeping a running tally of votes. Once she'd gotten past her nerves that first day, she seemed to get a kick out of the process of trying out dishes and getting feedback. Camila had no doubt soon her dishes would be favorites at the restaurant.

"Guess I'm free to go." Camila let Carl lead her to the door. In his truck, as he drove them toward the edge of town, she asked, "What's this all about?" She couldn't help reaching over and touching his arm. He took her hand and held it as he drove, rubbing his thumb over her palm until her body thrummed with need. Twice they'd managed to be together, slipping off in Carl's truck and finding quiet places to park off the road. But Camila was afraid sooner or later they'd get caught like that. The danger added a little thrill, but she was ready to spend a whole night with him.

"Soon," he kept saying whenever she spoke that desire out loud.

She wondered what he was waiting for. She didn't want to leave Juana alone too much so soon after she'd arrived, but her cousin could stand a single night alone in the cabin.

"It's a surprise."

He turned on the radio and hummed along to a country song. Sunshine flooded the truck cab, raising Camila's spirits. She loved spending time with him no matter what they did, and life was good with Juana fitting in so well at the restaurant and her parents happy about their impending move. Even Mateo seemed upbeat these days, sending her texts about his plans for turning the restaurant into a nightclub. He kept sending her lists of bands he wanted to book. She had high hopes for how that would turn out.

"While we have a minute, I've got a question," Carl said.

"Fire away."

"I thought you grew up in Mexico."

Camila bit her lip. Here it was, the topic she'd been dreading. But this was Carl. He'd come clean about the secrets he was keeping. It was her turn.

"I lied," she said.

"Why?"

"When I first got here, I thought people wouldn't take me seriously as the owner of a Mexican restaurant unless I was from Mexico. I was having a bit of a crisis. Leaving home—it was harder than I'd thought."

Carl nodded. "I guess I've seen and heard enough these past few days to understand why you'd feel that way. Are you going to tell your friends?"

She thought about that. "I guess so. They aren't going to care one bit, are they?"

"Nope." He chuckled, and she thought about Juana, hiding her desire to come to the United States out of fear of what her parents would think—and then learning her mother meant to send her here whether she wanted to go or not.

"Life is weird," Camila said. "We spend a lot of time worrying about the wrong things."

"You've said a mouthful."

Camila straightened when Carl turned into a driveway, pressed a button on a remote control to make a gate open and continued on, stopping only when the grounds opened up to reveal a ranch spreading all around them.

"What do you think?" he asked.

"It's lovely. Is it for sale?" She couldn't let herself hope it was. This wasn't just an average ranch; it was a stunning property.

"Not anymore."

Her heart sank. Of course not. But this was the kind of ranch Carl wanted—that must be what he'd brought her here to see. Something to hope for in the future—

"I bought it last week. Just cleared escrow this morning." He held up a key. "Want to take a look?"

Camila's breath caught. "You bought it?"

"Yep." He was grinning ear to ear.

"You really bought it?" she asked again. "And it's yours? No tricks? No way to lose it again?"

"It's mine. Ours, someday, I hope. Do you like it?"

"Carl—it's beautiful!"

"The house needs work to make it a real home, but I think you'll like it." He drove the rest of the way up the drive and parked. "Come and see." When they reached the front porch, he unlocked the door and led the way inside. Camila gasped when she took in the view from the living room's floor-to-ceiling windows. The kitchen was something out of a dream: miles of stone countertops, a huge island with seats for eight. An eight-burner professional stove. She turned in a circle, trying to take it all in—.

But came to a stop, tears stinging her eyes when she caught sight of Carl down on one knee, a small velvet box in his hand. The cowboy grinned up at her.

"Camila, I know I should wait. I know we need to date, get to know each other, plan and dream—and I'm okay doing all those things. But please—say you'll marry me when we've done all that. I can't deal with the suspense any longer."

Camila couldn't answer. She hadn't realized until this moment how afraid she'd been that they'd never get here. Her hands were shaking. She couldn't seem to catch her breath. A tear spilled down her cheek.

"Camila?" Carl reached for her hand, and she laughed a little, nervousness overtaking her. "Hey," he said. "You're not supposed to laugh at me. You're not supposed to cry, either."

"I'm not laughing at you. I'm laughing at… life. It's so good," she managed to say through her tears. "I didn't know it could be so good."

He surged to his feet and caught her in his arms. She went up on tiptoe to kiss him. She couldn't believe how lucky she was—not that someone like Carl would fall for her, but that he loved her enough to wait until she was ready.

"You didn't answer my question," he finally said when he pulled back. "Will you marry me?"

She was making him wait again. "Yes," Camila told him. "Yes, I will marry you." She threw her arms around his neck and kissed him. She'd gladly marry him—right now if he had an officiant hidden somewhere.

"It's my huge-ass house, isn't it?" he asked when they broke apart some time later. "I mean, who could resist this?" He gestured to the enormous kitchen island.

"Not me," Camila said. "But it isn't the huge-ass house. It's the man. I love you."

"I love you, too." Carl took a ring out of the box. "You didn't even look at this yet." He slipped it onto her finger.

Camila gasped. The diamond-studded ring he'd chosen was exquisite. She felt like a princess wearing it. As he encircled her in his arms again, she had a feeling Carl would always make her feel that way.

He loved her.

And he'd put down roots here—he'd bought a ranch. Her ranch soon.

"I can barely take all this in," she said. "Why didn't you tell me about this place?"

"I had to make absolutely sure Virginia couldn't take it away again. She's the one who helped me find it."

"You think she would try to stop the deal if she knew you were with me?"

"Yes. Just to be ornery," he said. "But now she can't hurt us ever again."

"Does that mean we're going to tell the Turners and Coopers about being engaged?"

"Hell, yeah. I'm going to tell everyone." He lifted her up and twirled her around. "I'm going to marry Camila Torres," he shouted.

Camila laughed. "You'd better drive me back to town. I've got to help with the lunch rush."

"Sure thing." He set her down and led her toward a wide set of stairs. "But first let me show you the master bedroom."

Chapter Nine

WHENEVER HE KISSED Camila, all Carl's troubles receded into the back of his mind. He couldn't believe it had taken so many years to get her into his arms. It hadn't taken much to persuade her to try out the king-size bed in their new master suite. Now she lay next to him, tucked in his arms, looking up at him with plain anticipation.

"I love being with you," he told her, sliding his hands up under her shirt until they spanned her rib cage, his thumbs resting against the underside of her breasts. She leaned into him, and he skimmed them higher, palming her softness, uttering a moan she echoed. She let him push her shirt off her shoulders, and he drank in the sight of her breasts encased in a lacy blush-red bra. Camila was all woman, her curves spilling over its confines. When she lifted her hands to his shirt, he tugged it over his head and tossed it aside.

She splayed her hands over his chest, and a wash of heat spread through him. Now that they'd started, he didn't want to stop. He'd meant to take his time exploring Camila's body, but he found his fingers at the button of her jeans, and when she didn't stop him, he freed it from its buttonhole. Camila's hands were fumbling at his waistline, and soon they were racing to undress. When they were naked, Carl knelt between her thighs, boxed her in with a hand to either side of her head, leaned down and kissed her, sucking in his breath at the electricity between them everywhere they touched. He trailed kisses over her mouth, her jaw, down the side of her neck and into the hollow at the base of her throat.

Camila lifted her hands over her head, arched back and wrapped her legs around his waist.

Carl didn't need a clearer invitation. As he positioned himself, Camila moaned, a soft sound that revved him up. He knew exactly how she felt. He craved this night and day. He moved slowly, pushing inside her, trying to savor every sensation as pleasure spread through him. Camila met each thrust with a lift of her hips, guided his mouth to her breast and moaned with pleasure at his touch. He was having a hard time holding back, but he paced himself until she showed him with the motion of her hips that she didn't want him to go slow. She urged him on, moved against him, opened up to him until he lost control.

They went over the edge together, both of them crying out, neither bothering to hold back until Carl finally collapsed on top of her, breathing hard.

"Camila," he managed to say.

She wriggled underneath him, and when he slid out of her and shifted to the side to take his weight off her, she followed him and cuddled against him. Carl turned onto his back, tucking Camila under his arm. Staring up at the ceiling, he didn't care what happened next. This was all he needed. The woman he loved.

Everything else would work itself out.

THIS WAS PARADISE, Camila decided.

The ranch was wonderful, but at the end of the day, all she needed was Carl. He was a miracle among men. He'd understood her need for time to be ready for a relationship. He'd waited until he could fulfill her wishes—and those of her family.

He touched her in a way that left her breathless with desire. Even now—so soon after making love—she wanted him inside her again.

She wished she'd understood how special he was back when she'd first made her ultimatum. Instead of pushing him away, she would have invited him into her life and they could have lived in a cave for all she cared.

Although this house was pretty special.

She settled against Carl and tried to picture their future together. How many mornings would she wake up just like this, by Carl's side, anticipating the day?

How many meals would she cook in her glorious new kitchen? How many Christmases would they celebrate—how many trees would they decorate in the grand living room?

She'd hardly dared dream that life could ever work out this way—that she could ever actually end up with Carl.

She turned to him. "I love you."

He brushed a kiss across her mouth. "I love you, too. Always have, I think. From the first time I saw you."

"Why?"

"Because of your laugh," he confessed. "Only some people are open enough to life to laugh like that. I wanted to know who you were—how you were brave enough to do that. Back then I was still holding back a bit. Burned by Lacey."

"But you asked me out."

"I did."

"And told me you were serious."

"Because I was. From that first moment, I knew I wanted you to be my wife."

She tried to take it in. "You waited for me."

"Camila, what else could I have done?"

She didn't have an answer for that except to kiss him and, when that wasn't enough, to pull him close and let him make love to her all over again.

This time they moved together slowly, building to a peak that left her shaking when her orgasm spent itself. Every time she was with Carl it was a miracle. She hadn't known it could be this good.

"We should be getting back," she said reluctantly.

"I know." Carl sat up, and she followed him, sighing with pleasure when he cupped one of her breasts and bent to give it a final kiss. "I could stay here forever," he groaned. "Just you and me. No clothes."

"Sounds heavenly."

"When should we tie the knot?" Carl asked Camila

as they dressed.

"Soon," she said.

Carl's pulse gave a throb. "Are you sure? We haven't exactly gotten a lot of chances to date." He didn't want to rush this. He intended to marry once, which meant he owed Camila a whole lot of romance, because he didn't want her ever to go looking for it from another man.

"I'm sure. Carl—I'm ready for this, does that make sense? I'm ready to be settled here. To move on with our lives, together."

Carl crossed to her and pulled her into an embrace. She felt so good fitted against his body. "How soon?"

"The first Saturday in June," she said.

"That's just weeks away!" He pulled back. "What about your family? Won't they need more warning than that? And we have to find a venue—"

"We'll hold it here," she said simply.

Of course. He should have thought of that.

"This week we'll make our plans. We'll do our invitations and make our lists. Next week we'll put it in motion and make it happen."

"Just like that?" he asked.

"Just like that. I own a restaurant, for heaven's sake, so we've got catering taken care of. We'll need a huge dinner service anyway for this house, so we can order that in the next few days. All we need is someone to perform the ceremony."

"I'll ask Reverend Halpern," Carl said. "Unless you'd prefer a priest."

"I like Reverend Halpern," she told him, "If we have a priest, we'd have to marry in church, and I want to marry on our front lawn."

"Your family won't mind?"

"It's our wedding," she told him. "That means we get to do what we want."

"Okay, I can agree to that." He leaned forward to kiss her forehead. "But are you sure?" he asked again.

"I've never been surer about anything." She reached up to kiss his cheek.

He pulled her close again. "You're going to make me the happiest man on earth."

"I'm going to try."

"YOU'RE GLOWING," JUANA said when Camila entered the restaurant again. She and Fila had gotten everything prepared, and the first of the lunch customers were just arriving. Camila hurried to wash her hands, tie on her apron and get to work, too.

Fila looked up at her. "Juana's right; you are glowing. What's going on?"

"Nothing. Just had a good time with Carl." She waved her hand to show off her ring, and Fila let out a gasp.

"He proposed?" She rushed over to look. "Oh, my goodness, that's a gorgeous ring!"

"Will you two be my bridesmaids?"

"Bridesmaids!" Fila's shriek must have been audible across town. "Yes, of course!"

"Absolutely!" Juana said. Both of them threw their

arms around Camila and hugged her.

"That's not all," Camila said. "Carl bought a ranch…"

Later that night, safe in her cabin, happier than she could say, Camila dialed her parents' phone number. She was tucked in her bed in comfy pajamas, Juana asleep already on the hide-a-bed in the living room.

"*Mamá?* It's me."

"*Cariña*, how are you? How's your cousin?"

"She's doing great. She keeps coming up with different burrito fillings, and everyone loves them. I think it's going to be her thing."

Her mother chuckled. "So she has had to adapt, like we have all had to."

"Was it hard for you and *Papá* when you first got to Houston?"

"*Sí.* So hard. We had to adapt, too," her mother said. "But I am glad we came. We learned so much."

Camila couldn't remember her mother ever being so positive.

"Now we return to Mexico at the end of June," Paula added. "We are helping Mateo renovate the restaurant and then we'll go home."

Home. Her mother said the word with all the reverence Camila had begun to feel for Chance Creek.

"You're going to love being back in Mexico, won't you?" she asked softly.

"*Sí.* I hadn't known how much I missed it. I'll still miss you, though. Maybe you'll come back, too, someday?"

"To visit," Camila told her. "But Chance Creek is my home now. *Mamá*, I'm going to marry Carl. And he bought a ranch. I'm going to have a home of my own."

"Cariña!" Her mother launched into an excited spate of Spanish, talking so fast Camila could barely keep up. "Diego. Diego! Camila is getting married!"

Camila had to laugh when her father got on the line, too.

"You're getting married?"

"Yes."

"To Carl?"

"Yes!"

She told them about their wedding plans and their new house.

"We'll have a guest room for you any time you want to visit." She bit her lip, remembering they'd never visited before. "You will come to the wedding, won't you?" she asked in a small voice.

"Of course we'll come. I'm the mother of the bride!"

"And I'm the father. I need to walk my girl down the aisle."

"And I need to cook!" her mother added.

Camila's heart swelled. "I can't wait to see you again."

"Neither can I," her mother said. "Now tell me everything."

IT WAS IRONIC that just a week ago Carl had stood onstage at the high school's auditorium and been excited to address the public. Tonight he was dreading facing the crowd who would gather soon at Fila's Familia. Now that he had the deed to Laurel Heights in his hand, he and Camila had decided it was time to announce their engagement—and upcoming wedding— to the Turners and Coopers.

They'd debated how best to do it, and Camila had made it clear she thought each of them should talk alone to their honorary "families." But Carl didn't want her facing the Turners without him. He figured they should get it all done at once.

"Do you think this is going to work?" Fila asked him. They were in the kitchen, the women working hard to prepare a special meal. They'd decided to close the restaurant to the public tonight and serve a banquet to the two families.

"Food soothes the savage beast, and all," Camila had said.

"That's music," Fila had told her dryly.

So now music was wafting through the restaurant as well. Soothing music from a mix Fila had found online at a New Age site. It was called *Harmonious Interweaving*. Carl hoped it worked.

"Smells good in here," Cab Johnson called out when he opened the door to the restaurant a few minutes later.

Carl pushed through the swinging kitchen door and went to meet him. "Thanks for coming."

"Thought about bringing the SWAT team along," Cab joked. "Figured that might be overkill, though."

"Maybe. Maybe not," Camila said, coming out of the kitchen, too, and wiping her hands on her apron. "Cab, good to see you again. Think you can keep the peace while we make our announcement?"

"I hope so."

"Maybe you should eat now," Fila said, following her. "You might be too busy later."

"I'll take an appetizer to tide me over," Cab agreed.

He was still eating an empanada when the door opened again and Jedidiah Turner walked in, followed by Noah, Liam, Maya and Stella. Camila greeted them warmly and ushered them to a table while Cab and Carl talked. Carl caught the Turners looking his way more than once, but they didn't seem to realize he was the reason they were there.

"What are we celebrating?" Jed kept asking.

"You'll see. It's a surprise," Camila told him.

"Is this about Juana?" Maya asked. "How is she doing?"

"Just great," Camila assured her. "She'll be out later. I need to go help, so relax and enjoy; I'll get drinks out to you shortly."

She disappeared into the kitchen, as they'd planned. A few moments later, the Coopers showed up.

"Virginia!" Carl met her at the door and ushered her into the restaurant. Steel, Lance and Olivia followed.

All of them stopped when they caught sight of the Turners sitting around a table.

"What's the meaning of this?" Virginia demanded of Carl.

"Have a seat." He indicated a table across the room from the Turners.

"Why are they here?" she asked, not moving an inch.

"I can't control who comes to a restaurant. But I can buy all of you dinner. So sit down, and let's get ready to order."

"This is a setup, isn't it?" Olivia demanded under her breath as she passed him on the way to the table. Carl heaved a sigh of relief when the Coopers were all sitting down.

Just as he and the women had planned, they began to bring out platters of food the minute everyone was seated. Cab sat at a small table placed between the two families. Fila served him first with a single platter lined with small portions from many of the dishes they served.

"This is our sampler platter," she told him and set it down with a flourish.

Juana followed with the drink he'd ordered, then both women went back to get more. Fila served the Coopers next, while Juana served the Turners.

"Aren't you going to sit?" Virginia asked.

"I've got something to say first." He waited until all the food and drinks were on the tables before he fetched Camila. He squeezed her hand as he led her back into the main room of the restaurant, and she squeezed his back.

A murmur of conversation ran around the room as both families took in the way they were standing together.

"Listen up, folks," Carl began. "I've got something to say. We both do." He took a deep breath. "Camila and I are getting married."

CAMILA HAD EXPECTED a reaction to their announcement, but this took the cake. Virginia and Jed both jumped to their feet, Jed yelling at Camila for her disloyalty, and Virginia yelling at him to shut up. Liam and Lance hurled insults at each other across the restaurant. Stella and Maya looked shocked, and Olivia and Noah seemed to be having some kind of secret communication with looks and shrugs.

Cab waited a long moment, got slowly to his feet and suddenly bellowed, "Shut up!"

In the stunned silence that followed, the sheriff wiped his hands on a napkin. "Those two are in love. Get over it."

"I helped that traitor buy a ranch," Virginia sputtered. "This is how he repays me?"

"I helped you ram your school project through the board's approval process," Carl reminded her. "We're even, as far as I see it."

"That's what happens when you try to outwit the Turners," Jed told Virginia. "You get your comeuppance."

"I'll come up your you-know-what in a minute and give you what-for!" Virginia retorted.

"Settle down!" Cab put his hands on his hips. "I've got two things to say to you all. One—" he held up a finger "—neither Carl nor Camila are Turners or Coopers."

The room erupted again until Cab slapped his hand on the table and they settled back down.

"Two, I haven't heard a single congratulations out of any of you. And that's just plain bad manners."

"It's bad manners to marry the enemy," Virginia said.

"Carl isn't my enemy." Camila spoke up for the first time. "He's a man I've loved for years. We invited you here because we hoped you'd come to our wedding, but that's not going to happen unless you can behave yourselves."

"Behave ourselves?" Liam spoke up. "You two are the ones sneaking around behind everyone's back. That's not well-behaved."

"That's self-preservation," Carl contradicted him. "And you know I'm right."

Liam subsided into muttered complaints.

"Look, we're marrying with or without you, and we're doing so at our new ranch," Carl said. "You want to get a good look at it, you'd better make your peace with us being together. Otherwise none of you gets an invite."

"It's going to be the wedding of the year," Camila proclaimed. "Good food, good drinks. Lots of music and dancing."

"I want to come to your wedding," Olivia said suddenly. "I'll behave myself. I swear."

Camila exchanged a glance with Carl. Progress.

"Olivia," Lance said warningly.

"Oh, come on," she told her brother. "It's a wedding. Carl and Camila are in love; anyone can see that. I'm not such a child that I can't behave for a day at a public occasion. Are you?"

"No," Lance said shortly.

"Then you'd better tell Carl and Camila that."

"Congratulations," Lance muttered. "I'll come to your wedding."

"We appreciate your enthusiasm," Carl told him.

"I'll come, too," Noah said, startling all of them. He hadn't said a word so far.

"Noah," Stella hissed.

"If a Cooper can do it, I can do it," he said. "You should, too." He turned to Carl and Camila. "Congratulations, you two. I hope you're very happy."

"Congratulations," Maya echoed him.

"Congratulations," Stella finally said, but she was looking at the table.

"Congrats," Liam muttered.

"Olivia's right," Steel said suddenly. "You two belong together and I, for one, am happy you found each other. I'd be glad to come to the wedding, too."

"Jed. Virginia. That leaves you two," Cab pointed out.

Virginia crossed her arms. "If the wedding is at the ranch I found for you, I suppose I might attend," she said snippily.

"If she's there, I'll come to make sure she doesn't steal anything, like that no good grand-niece of hers."

Jed jutted his chin at Olivia, who rolled her eyes.

"Then it's all settled," Cab said. "Everyone dig in before your food gets cold." He sat down and commenced eating, lifting his glass to Carl and Camila when everyone else followed suit.

AFTER HIS FAILURE to help his friend negotiate his deal with Fulsom, Carl felt bad asking Sven not only to travel to attend his wedding, but also to be the best man. But Sven seemed to think nothing of it. He was so happy about how the buyout had gone, Carl suspected he'd forgive anything just then.

Now Carl's wedding day had arrived, and Sven stood by while he got ready, ostensibly for moral support, but to Carl's surprise he didn't feel any anxiety. He'd assumed wedding jitters were inevitable, like death and taxes, but as he looked in the mirror, he realized he'd never been more certain he was doing the right thing.

"Guess I'm about as presentable as I'll ever be," he said, giving his tie one final tug. He glanced at his watch. "Promised Camila I'd be out of the house pretty quick. Let's walk the grounds."

Even after the weeks he'd lived here, there was still plenty of ground left to walk. The fresh morning air and scents of flowering trees called him back to when he'd walked the Pacific Crest Trail years ago, and he smiled when he thought of how far he'd come since then. Glancing at his friend walking beside him, he realized the years had been even more transformative for Sven.

"What are you thinking?" Sven asked. "You're grinning like a loon."

"The past few years felt like an eternity. Can't begin to count how many times I've thought I would never find a ranch, never get to date Camila, never fit in here. Looking back on it from this end? It's amazing how fast it's all gone. Now everything's changed, and I've got the life I want."

Sven nodded. "Know what you mean."

They met up with some of Camila's relatives near the pavilion where the ceremony was to be held. Arturo and Luis both greeted him warmly. Carl introduced them to Sven, and they continued the tour of the grounds together.

"You'll have to visit us again soon," Carl said to Camila's brothers, who were only there for a couple of days. "Maybe come and help me with the place now and then."

They both nodded. "We might as well," Luis said. "*Tío* Diego keeps saying he's going to do all the ranch work in Guerrero himself. We keep telling him he'll have to take it easy, given his health, but just thinking about it is doing him good. The doctor says his blood pressure is down. I swear he lost five pounds overnight."

"The problem was indeed in his heart," Arturo said, placing a hand on his chest. "But not in the way the doctors thought. Now that he knows he's coming home, he's a happy man."

Luis surveyed the landscape. "This is a strange

ranch. I'm used to fewer cows and a lot more corn."

"I'm glad you brought that up. I've been thinking about trying something new with this property. Camila and I are both very busy people, and we both like it that way. I can't give up ranching, and I'd never ask her to give up her restaurant, but I don't like the way the most important parts of our lives are so separate. I want to bring them more in line. Camila and Juana are trying to add authentic Mexican dishes to the menu, but it's hard for them to get the right ingredients. What they need is an authentic Mexican ranch."

Arturo scratched his chin. "A novel idea. But do not tell me you mean to grow mangoes and poblano peppers in Montana? I do not see it."

Carl nodded. "That's exactly what I mean. You'd be amazed what you can do with geothermal technology these days. This place has more outbuildings than a normal ranch could ever need, and a lot of it was built with aesthetics in mind rather than functionality. See that extra stable over there, with all the glasswork? You'd be insane to put horses in there, but it'd make a fine greenhouse. Not saying it will be easy, but that's the point. I'm not happy unless my mind is working as hard as my hands." He smiled at Luis and Arturo. "Of course, I don't know the first thing about Mexican ranching—except not to let the cows head for the river till after it rains." They all laughed. "To do this right, I'll need some help."

"I'll help," Arturo said.

"Me, too."

"You'd need heat and light in the winter," Sven mused, sizing up the building in question. "And open air in spring for pollination... some sort of retractable roof...? On an automated schedule, timed—no, with ambient sensors, powered by a solar array..."

Carl fought to suppress a smile. His trap had worked. After all, Sven had just sold his company. Soon enough he'd need something new to do. Still, he proceeded cautiously. "I'd hate to ask you to jump into anything, seeing as you—"

Sven cut him off. "Are you kidding? I was so busy trying to get rich and retire young I never thought about what I'd do afterward." He shook his head. "Took me about two hours to get sick of relaxing by the pool. I'm already restless. I lie awake at night dreaming up schematics and prototypes. It's all I can do to keep myself from taking apart and optimizing my toaster every morning."

Carl raised his eyebrows. "You're a freshly minted millionaire, and you still eat toast for breakfast? Besides, I know darn well it'll be months before the hand-over is complete."

"Please, Carl, I need something new to think about. I'm begging you!"

"All right, all right!" Carl threw up his hands in mock exasperation. "If it means that much to you, I'll let you build me a revolutionary geothermic mango grow-op the likes of which the world has never seen. But you'd better not make a mess."

MIDAFTERNOON, CAMILA STOOD by the window in one of several guest rooms in Carl's new—no, in *their* new home. To keep Carl from seeing her in her wedding dress, they'd agreed she would remain inside, and he outside, until the ceremony. She'd been busy overseeing the preparations, but now, with everything done, she ached to be outdoors. Not just because of the brilliant sunshine and the beautiful grounds, but because she couldn't stand to be away from Carl.

She frowned as she took in the pure blue sky. True, it was a blessing for her wedding day, but a lot of folk in town were beginning to worry. Since there'd been plenty of rain in Guerrero, Camila hadn't realized anything was amiss back here in Chance Creek at first, but she'd learned there hadn't been any rain the whole time she'd been gone—or any since.

She'd worry about that another day, she resolved. For now she was content to count her blessings. She had Carl, and they had the perfect ranch. Through their new menu items at Fila's, she was continuing to reconnect with her heritage, and the citizens of Chance Creek were enthusiastic about it. Carl had wrapped up his business in California and didn't have any reason to leave Montana any time soon. Perhaps most miraculously, her whole family had come to celebrate this milestone in her life.

She smiled as her eyes drifted to where a pavilion had been set up, along with rows of chairs. They'd talked her relatives down from throwing them an authentic Mexican wedding—the groom barely spoke

Spanish, after all—but had allowed them to add a few touches. The aisle between the chairs had been strewn with bright purple jacaranda petals. And of course, mounted prominently above where she and Carl would soon say their vows, was the Olmec jade face mask that started this whole crazy adventure.

"There's the bride. How do you feel?"

Camila glanced back and smiled to see Mateo entering the room. "Never better," she told him honestly.

"I need to thank you."

"No, you don't," she began, but Mateo cut her off.

"Yes, I do. I missed you when you moved away, you know. But I have to admit I was glad you never came back and upstaged me."

"I never meant to make you feel bad," Camila said. "All I wanted was to cook."

"I know. It's what you were born to do. And what I was born *having* to do." A trace of old bitterness crossed Mateo's face, but then he grinned. "Now I get to do what I'm really good at: being the life of the party. *Papá* approved my business plan before we left Houston."

"That's wonderful!" Camila wrapped her brother in her arms, and he hugged her back with enthusiasm.

"It took some convincing. You know how he is about stereotyping Mexican culture. I plan to capitalize on everything that's hip and sexy about Mexico: salsa dancing, *sangrita*, *reggaeton*, wild colors, spicy appetizers. At first *Papá* insisted it would give gringos a narrow view of our heritage. I convinced him that even though those things are a tiny part of our culture and there's so much more than that, they still are part of Mexico. If I can get people to take that first bite, maybe they'll want to look a little deeper, no?" He laughed. "Besides, I showed him how you can sell the same plate of *queso fundido* at a bar for three times what people would pay for it at dinner—and much more for drinks, too. My projections show a lot more profit than we ever had as a restaurant. I'm sure that helped sway him."

"It sounds amazing! I'll have to come visit." Camila had never seen Mateo so excited about anything.

"You can do a lot more than that, if you want. Someone still needs to make that *queso fundido* after all."

Camila blinked. "Are you… offering me a job?"

"Something like that. Don't think of it as working for me, though. You'd be kitchen manager, and I'd give you full reign to run things however you wanted. I want this club to be the best of the best, and I can't think of anyone better to make sure our food is up to that standard."

Camila didn't know what to say. Years of insecurity, resentment and doubt washed away in a moment. After a lifetime of taking second place to her brother, here he was telling her she was the best.

But it only took another moment before she shook her head. "It means the world to me, really, that you asked. But I know now more than ever that Chance Creek is my home. What?"

Mateo was nodding along and smiling even as she spoke. "I know. You've built an incredible life for yourself here—I didn't really have high hopes."

"Then why offer?"

"Because I wanted you to know that you deserve it. You always have."

She hugged him again.

"You'll be a part of it, in a small way," Mateo said when they broke apart. "None of this would be possible if not for you and Carl, and I wanted to honor that. Seeing as the name Torres de Sabores doesn't really suit a nightclub, I'm going to change it to Oro y Plata."

Camila frowned. *Gold and Silver?* A decent name, she supposed, but she wasn't sure what it had to do with her and Carl. "I don't get it."

"I do," Fila said as she came in grinning. "It's Montana's state motto, silly." She took Mateo's arm. "You have another visitor, Camila. Come on, let's give them some privacy."

Fila and Mateo left, and a moment later Camila's father entered. Diego hesitated in the doorway. "Big day," he said finally.

She nodded.

"I wanted to tell you how proud I am of you today. And… always."

Camila didn't know what to do. When her father crossed the room and embraced her, she hugged him back, blinking away her tears before they spoiled her makeup.

"Is there anything I can do for you?" he asked when they broke apart again. "Must be a hectic day."

"There is one thing." Camila took a deep breath. "Ever since going to Mexico I've been wondering about my name. Mexicans traditionally have at least four. Why do I only have three?"

"Your mother and I agreed that all of our children born in America should have names that conform to American standards—at least legally. You might only have three names on your passport, but in our hearts you have always had four."

"Really?"

"By Mexican convention, your paternal last name would be Torres, and your maternal last name would be Barrera. And of course your second name is Margarita."

"Right," Camila said. "So my name is…"

"Camila Margarita Torres Barrera." Her father smiled, glancing out at the pavilion outside. "At least for a few more hours."

Chapter Ten

"HERE WE GO," Sven said, taking his place by Carl's side on the raised dais at the end of the aisle.

"Don't get all weepy on me, Andersson," Carl teased.

"No promises."

All eyes turned to the back of the aisle as music filled the air. Sitting at an upright piano the men had painstakingly dragged out here that morning, Savannah Cook played the wedding march as first Fila, then Juana, walked down the aisle in their beautiful, wine-red bridesmaid gowns. Then Diego came out, looking proud as hell with Camila on his arm, who wore stunning white gown that fit her curves. Its bodice was covered in lace, a traditional touch to a modern dress. It suited Camila perfectly.

For the first time all day Carl felt a pang of anxiety. Not that he was making the wrong choice, but that maybe Camila was. Watching her walk toward him, so regal she almost seemed to float, he despaired of ever living up to this breathtaking woman who had somehow agreed to spend her life with him. Casting a glance at

Ximena in the front row, he almost wished he'd brought a bottle of mezcal to the altar with him to steady his sudden nerves.

The moment Camila took her place across from him, however, the feeling vanished. He looked into her eyes and saw the love he felt for her reflected back at him. Carl thought nothing had ever been so right. Of course they were meant to be together.

He took her hand as the reverend began to speak.

CAMILA THOUGHT CARL had never looked more handsome than he did standing at the altar beside her. He stood tall and straight, and his hand holding hers kept her nerves at bay. This was the way they'd take on life—together. Supporting each other. Facing whatever came side by side.

She couldn't wait.

Behind her sat her friends and family—and even the Turners and the Coopers were behaving themselves. When Reverend Halpern began to speak the traditional words of the marriage ceremony, her heart beat hard and fast, but her words came out clear and strong, and she'd never meant anything so utterly as she did when she said her vows.

When it was over, Carl swept her into an embrace and kissed her like he'd never let go again.

"I love you," he told her.

"I love you, too."

They barely made it back up the aisle before they were swamped with well-wishers, and soon the band they'd hired had struck up a tune and Juana and the others were setting out a huge buffet of food.

It all felt like a dream to Camila, and she kept wondering if the clock would strike twelve and it would all disappear.

"Congratulations," Noah said, appearing at her side and handing her a glass of champagne. "I'm really happy for you, Camila."

"You don't think I'm a traitor to the Turners?"

"No." He sighed. "I wish this stupid feud had never started."

She noticed his gaze rest on Olivia Cooper but bit back the question that sprang to her lips. She hoped for Noah's sake he hadn't formed an attachment to Olivia. Their families might let her and Carl get away with being together, but they'd never stand for one of their own to cross the boundary between them.

"Maybe it will settle down someday."

Noah made a face. "Not sure that's likely any time soon. Congratulations again, though."

"Thank you." She spotted Carl talking to a knot of Coopers. "Think you all can make it through the night without coming to blows?"

"Here's hoping." Noah clinked his champagne glass with hers and downed its contents in one long gulp.

"IT'S NOT THE same without you around Thorn Hill," Olivia said to Carl when they met up at the buffet table.

"I didn't move that far away," he reminded her.

"Sure feels like it. I'm used to seeing you on a daily

basis."

"Maybe someone better will move into your cabin now I'm gone."

"Maybe." Her gaze drifted toward Noah Turner, and Carl wondered what she was thinking.

"How are things on the ranch?"

"Dry."

"Same here," he said. "Hope the rains come soon."

"I think everyone's hoping that. Maybe your marriage to Camila will bring some luck to us all."

"I sure hope so. Speaking of Camila, I'd better get back to her."

"I'm glad you married her, Carl. For real," Olivia added. "I'm glad our stupid feud with the Turners didn't mess things up for you two."

"Maybe it's time you all buried the hatchet," he suggested.

Olivia rolled her eyes. "Do you think that's likely?"

"We can always hope for a miracle, right?"

"LET'S NOT EVER pick a fight with our neighbors," Camila said later that night when she and Carl were dancing their first dance together.

"Funny, I was thinking the same thing," Carl said and stole a kiss.

"We're going to make a good life here, aren't we?"

"You better believe we are." He told her about Arturo, Luis and Sven all wanting to come and help.

"I have a feeling we're always going to have company at the house."

"Good thing it's a big house. Sometimes I'm going to want to have you to myself." His arms tightened around her, and Camila leaned against his chest.

"I'm going to want that, too."

"Sooner rather than later, preferably."

Camila laughed. "Let's enjoy the party first."

A few minutes later, her parents joined them on the dance floor, and then more couples came. Soon they were dancing in a sea of swaying bodies, as the sun went down and the moon lit the sky.

"Everything's perfect," Camila said, looking up and taking it all in.

"You're right; everything is perfect," Carl said, his gaze steady on her.

Camila wondered if she'd ever stop feeling this much love for her husband. She doubted it, she thought, as he bent to kiss her.

And then all she could think about was Carl.

To find out more, look for *The Cowboy's Outlaw Bride*,
Volume 2 in the *Turners v. Coopers* series.

Be the first to know about Cora Seton's new releases!
Sign up for her newsletter here!
www.coraseton.com/sign-up-for-my-newsletter

Other books in the Turners v. Coopers Series:

The Cowboy's Outlaw Bride (Volume 2)
The Cowboy's Hidden Bride (Volume 3)
The Cowboy's Stolen Bride (Volume 4)
The Cowboy's Forbidden Bride (Volume 5)

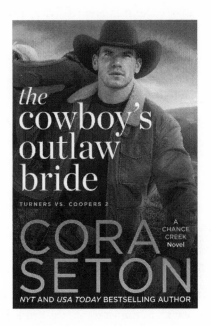

Read on for an excerpt of
The Cowboy's Outlaw Bride.

I T WOULD BE a miracle if this wedding didn't end with a fistfight.

Noah Turner watched Carl Whitfield waltz with his new bride, Camila, alone on the temporary dance floor built in the front yard of the Whitfields' new ranch. Surrounded by friends and family, it was clear they saw no one but each other. They deserved their happiness as far as Noah was concerned, but judging by the sour expression on his uncle Jed's face—and the looks and attitudes of the rest of the Turners and Coopers present—not everyone wished Carl and Camila well.

Carl had made the mistake of living for three years on Cooper land, renting a cabin from them at Thorn Hill, their extensive ranch. Camila had rented a cabin on Turner land at the Flying W for just as long. As far as Noah's uncle was concerned, Carl could be a Cooper himself, which made his marriage to Camila, an honorary Turner in Jed's mind, insupportable.

It would be funny if everyone wasn't taking it so damn seriously. Noah was keeping an especially close eye on his brother, Liam, who was glaring across the dance floor at Lance Cooper. Those two were apt to throw down whenever they met up. Noah wished they'd get over whatever had caused all that animosity between them, but the feud had stood between the Turners and Coopers for over a hundred years, and it obviously wasn't going to end tonight.

Which made it impossible for him to ask Olivia Cooper to dance.

He wanted to, though. Badly enough it took all his strength to stay where he was.

Olivia looked beautiful tonight in a short, light-blue off-the-shoulder dress. Her long legs were encased in cowboy boots. Her blonde hair done up in a twist. She looked sassy and sexy, and Noah couldn't keep his eyes off her.

No surprise: he could never look away when Olivia was around.

Everything had conspired to make this night a wonderful celebration for the newlyweds. The air was soft and warm. The evening sky glowed with an early June sunset. Stars were beginning to light up overhead one by one. The murmur of the other guests and the sweet melody of the string quartet provided a backdrop for the swaying couple. Noah wished he could relax and enjoy the occasion, but happy endings belonged to people like Carl and Camila, not people like him. Carl was a millionaire, and every inch of his new ranch oozed prosperity.

The Flying W didn't look half as good these days. Noah's family had fallen on hard times, and no matter how hard he worked, he couldn't seem to get them out from under their bills. He envied Carl the partner he'd gained in this wedding, too. Camila wasn't wealthy, but she had a good head on her shoulders, worked hard and obviously loved her new husband. What would it be like to have someone to share your life with? Someone on your side the way Camila seemed committed to Carl?

His own parents' marriage hadn't worked out, and that's when the fortunes of his family had turned. His mother had decamped to Ohio. His father died a few years back. Now Noah, the oldest of his siblings, was left in charge.

He was making a mess of the job. How could he expect any woman to want to be with him if he couldn't get it together?

His gaze slid to Olivia again. She was talking with her great-aunt Virginia on the other side of the dance floor, a stern old woman with upright bearing who carried an old black umbrella wherever she went. It was in her hand now. It was closed, and she was using it like a cane, leaning on it for support. She looked frustrated—or maybe *thwarted* was a better word. She didn't approve of this wedding any more than Noah's uncle Jed did.

Olivia was far more animated, talking rapidly, gesturing at the dancing couple. Trying to convince her aunt of something. Noah sighed, shoving his hands in the pockets of his good jeans. Much as he was attracted to Olivia, if he married someday, it couldn't be to her.

The Coopers had been his family's enemies since 1882, when Ernestine Harris jilted Olivia's great, great, great, great-grandfather, Slade Cooper, and married Noah's great, great, great, great-grandfather, Zeke Turner, instead. The feud between their families had been renewed when Virginia and Jed had a falling out in their early twenties. Then there was the trouble thirteen years ago…

Noah didn't like to think about that. He still wasn't sure exactly what had happened, except Olivia's father, Dale, had landed in jail, and her mother, Enid, had taken her and her siblings to Idaho for nearly a decade, leaving them with her sister when she ran off with a man and settled in New Mexico.

His own mother, Mary, had left home soon after Dale was arrested. Sometimes the disintegration of his and Olivia's families seemed linked in his mind, but it was only coincidence that it happened at the same time. Olivia's dad didn't live long enough to serve out his term. Noah's own father, William, died soon after. Even though the family rivalry hadn't caused this set of problems, the old feud was still in effect. His great-uncle Jed constantly bickered with Olivia's great-aunt Virginia at the Prairie Garden assisted living facility where they both lived. His brother, Liam, got into fisticuffs with Olivia's brother Lance with depressing regularity.

Thank goodness her sister, Tory, had decamped for Seattle years ago, or who knew what kind of arguments she'd have with his sister Stella. As for his youngest sister, Maya, who was near to Olivia's age, she and Olivia pretended each other didn't exist.

They were like Capulets and Montagues, Crips and Bloods... or, more apt, Hatfields and McCoys.

Which made it damn awkward he couldn't seem to get Olivia off his mind these days.

What did she think about him?

Did she ever think about him at all?

Noah settled his hat more firmly on his head. Probably not. Hell, he'd caught Olivia breaking and entering into his own house just a couple of weeks ago. She wouldn't do that if she liked him, would she?

He suppressed a smile. Actually, when he'd caught her she hadn't been in too much of a hurry to get away. In fact, she'd almost let him drive her to the Spring Fling Fair, except his family had arrived and all hell had broken loose.

Maybe she did like him a little bit.

But that didn't make their situation any better.

She clearly wasn't pleased with whatever her great-aunt was saying now. Noah edged sideways to get a better look. Virginia stood tapping the ground with her umbrella, giving Olivia what-for. As Noah watched, Olivia rolled her eyes and crossed her arms over her chest. Noah wondered what had riled up those two.

Not that it took much to rile a Cooper.

"What do you think that's about?" Maya appeared at his elbow and offered him a plate that held several kinds of dessert. Noah waved it off, and she shrugged, scooping up a bite of cake with her fork. Almost a foot shorter than him, with light brown hair and a pert nose, she stood on tiptoe to try to see. It was obvious she'd been watching the Coopers, too. She might ignore Olivia in public, but privately she seemed awfully interested in what Olivia got up to.

"Who knows?" He didn't want Maya to catch on that he was awfully interested, too.

"Life would be a whole lot more peaceful if they hadn't come back to town." She stabbed her fork into the cake again.

"Don't say that."

"Why not?"

Noah thought fast. "Thorn Hill is their home, just like the Flying W is ours. Must have been hard enough for them to stay away as long as they did."

What would Maya say if she knew who'd kept the lights on at Thorn Hill the whole time the Coopers were away? It sure had been a surprise to him when Lucas Maynard, the family's solicitor, took him aside after his father's death to explain the job his father had passed on to him. Noah still didn't understand why William was caught up in Cooper affairs.

This wasn't the time for that conversation, though. His father had wished to keep the arrangement a secret, and it was all done now—the Coopers were back at Thorn Hill, running it themselves. He'd keep his mouth shut and spend the rest of his life wondering what had happened thirteen years ago to make partners of two men who'd spent their lives on opposite sides of a family feud.

"You're always so fair," Maya chided him. "Anyway, it doesn't matter what we think about it. They're here now."

End of Excerpt

The Marine's E-Mail Order Bride (Volume 3)
The Navy SEAL's Christmas Bride (Volume 4)
The Airman's E-Mail Order Bride (Volume 5)

The SEALs of Chance Creek Series:

A SEAL's Oath

A SEAL's Vow

A SEAL's Pledge

A SEAL's Consent

A SEAL's Purpose

A SEAL's Resolve

A SEAL's Devotion

A SEAL's Desire

A SEAL's Struggle

A SEAL's Triumph

The Brides of Chance Creek Series:

Issued to the Bride One Navy SEAL
Issued to the Bride One Airman
Issued to the Bride One Sniper
Issued to the Bride One Marine
Issued to the Bride One Soldier

The Turners v. Coopers Series:

The Cowboy's Secret Bride (Volume 1)
The Cowboy's Outlaw Bride (Volume 2)
The Cowboy's Hidden Bride (Volume 3)
The Cowboy's Stolen Bride (Volume 4)
The Cowboy's Forbidden Bride (Volume 5)

About the Author

NYT and USA Today bestselling author Cora Seton loves cowboys, hiking, gardening, bike-riding, and lazing around with a good book. Mother of four, wife to a computer programmer/backyard farmer, she recently moved to Victoria and looks forward to a brand new chapter in her life. Like the characters in her Chance Creek series, Cora enjoys old-fashioned pursuits and modern technology, spending mornings in her garden, and afternoons writing the latest Chance Creek romance novel. Visit **www.coraseton.com** to read about new releases, contests and other cool events!

Blog:

www.coraseton.com

Facebook:

www.facebook.com/coraseton

Twitter:

www.twitter.com/coraseton

Newsletter:

www.coraseton.com/sign-up-for-my-newsletter

44477650R00154

Made in the USA
Middletown, DE
07 May 2019